Egbert P. Watson

A Manual of the Hand Lathe

SALZWASSER VERLAG

Egbert P. Watson

A Manual of the Hand Lathe

1st Edition | ISBN: 978-3-75250-165-0

Place of Publication: Frankfurt am Main, Germany

Year of Publication: 2020

Salzwasser Verlag GmbH, Germany.

Reprint of the original, first published in 1869.

A
MANUAL

OF THE

HAND LATHE:

COMPRISING

CONCISE DIRECTIONS

FOR

WORKING METALS OF ALL KINDS, IVORY, BONE AND PRECIOUS
WOODS; DYEING, COLORING, AND FRENCH POLISHING;
INLAYING BY VENEERS, AND VARIOUS METHODS
PRACTICED TO PRODUCE ELABORATE WORK
WITH DISPATCH, AND AT SMALL EXPENSE.

BY EGBERT P. WATSON,

LATE OF "THE SCIENTIFIC AMERICAN," AUTHOR OF "THE MODERN PRACTICE OF
AMERICAN MACHINISTS AND ENGINEERS."

ILLUSTRATED BY SEVENTY-EIGHT ENGRAVINGS.

PHILADELPHIA:
HENRY CAREY BAIRD, INDUSTRIAL PUBLISHER,
406 WALNUT STREET.
LONDON:
SAMPSON LOW, SON & MARSTON,
CROWN BUILDINGS, 188 FLEET ST.
1869.

TO MY DEAR SON,

EGBERT PERLEY WATSON,

I DEDICATE

THIS LITTLE BOOK,

IN THE

HOPE THAT HE MAY BE A GOOD MAN,

AND A GOOD MECHANIC.

PREFACE.

I DID not write this little book with the intention of apologizing to the prospective reader, so soon as I had done so, but with the honest, I hope not egotistical, feeling that I had something to say that was not generally known. We live to learn and to impart what we know to others, and I have taken this method of giving my experience in a pastime that is elevating, artistic in every sense of the word, and a wholesome relief from the cares of business.

In regard to the work itself, I can show samples of every thing of any importance described or given in it. I have not made all of the patterns given in the back part, for that is mere routine, but in gross, and in most details, the book is the result of experience, and will be found reliable *as far as it goes.* That it does not cover every possible change and use to which the lathe can be put, I am well aware.

Something must be left for the workman to find out himself. Neither have I given any recipes for varnishes, for those cannot be made by inexperienced persons. Moreover, they can be had so cheaply and universally, that it is mere folly for any amateur to make them.

Saluting all persons who love the art of which this little volume is descriptive,

I am their sincere friend,

EGBERT P. WATSON.

New York, *April* 15, 1869.

CONTENTS.

CHAPTER X.

CHAPTER XI.

CHAPTER XII.

CHAPTER XIII.

CHAPTER XIV.

CHAPTER XV.

CHAPTER XVI.

MANUAL
OF THE HAND LATHE.

CHAPTER I.

THE FOOT LATHE.

THERE are two distinct kinds of work done in foot lathes—the useful and the merely ornamental. Both afford enjoyment and profit to those who practise them. The mechanic who earns his living by working ten hours a day in a workshop, does not care to go home and pursue the same calling in the evening; but he can institute an agreeable change in his life, beautify his dwelling, and cultivate his taste, by the use of the lathe, and thus obtain ornaments that would cost large sums if purchased at the stores; or he may, indeed, make the lathe a source of revenue, and sell the product of his skill and ingenuity at high prices to those who admire, but have not the ability to construct.

To many mechanics, even, the lathe is merely a machine for turning cylinders or disks, or exe-

2

cuting beads, ogees, scrolls, or curves of various radii, so that, after all, the work is pretty much alike, and ceases to be attractive. This is quite a mistaken view. There are no such goods in market as those made on lathes, and peculiar tools used in connection with them—by lathes with traversing mandrels, with geometric chucks, with dome chucks, and compound slide rests. There are lathes that, while one could chase up a five-eight bolt in them as well as on the simple pulley and treadle machine, are also capable of executing all sorts of beautiful things—vases with bases nearly square, or exactly square, with round tops and hexagonal bodies, with gracefully-curved angular sides and bases, fluted vertically; boxes with curious patterns, resembling basket work; in fact, any combination of straight and curved lines, cut in the sides, it is possible for an ingenious man to invent. Strictly speaking, these are not lathes, for in order to do the things before mentioned it is necessary to use after attachments in connection with them, so that the combination of them produces the results spoken of. There is, absolutely, an unlimited field for the genius of workmen to exert itself in designing patterns and executing work of an ornamental character.

All ornamental work resolves itself into movements of three kinds—angular, circular and straight. From the combination of these with each other, the times where they merge and emerge, where a movement of one kind changes into any other, where an ellipse becomes part of a circle, where circles are generated across the circumferences of other circles, where these patterns are drawn over and upon each other without destroying the character of either—we say, by such movements, and many others which it would be confusing to follow, the most beautiful forms are made.

Or, if the taste of the workman runs upon mechanical instead of artistic things, there are steam engines to be made, steam boilers to be spun up, of small size; in fact, any piece or machine that can be thought of.

It is almost unnecessary to specify the innumerable kinds of work that can be done in a hand lathe, but the amateur who delights in metal turning may make trinkets of all kinds for his friends, that shall vie in beauty with the best efforts of the jeweler and goldsmith. This, of course, is dependent on the material used, the taste of the workman, and his originality of conception. Pins for ladies' wear can be made of boxwood and ebony, glued together in sections, of all designs, and afterwards turned in beads and mouldings, or otherwise ornamented in a chuck, as will be

shown hereafter. Sleeve buttons can be made of
ebony and silver, ivory and silver, pearl and gold,
or any combination that is desired. Chess and
checker men also afford a chance to display skill.
And, besides these, special work of any nature is
within the capacity of the machine.

There is no family in this country that would
not find it economy to have a foot lathe in the
house, where the members have mechanical tastes
—not necessarily the male members, for ladies use
foot lathes, in Europe, with the greatest dexterity.
Some of the most beautiful work ever made, was
by Miss Holtzapfel, a relative of the celebrated
mechanist of the same name. If there are shovels
to be mended, the lathe will drill the holes and
turn the rivets. If the handle of the saucepan is
loose, it will do the same. If scissors or knives
want grinding, there is the lathe; if the castors on
the sofa break down, there is the lathe; if skates
need repairs, either of grinding or of any other
kind, there is the lathe. In short, it ought to be
as much a part of domestic economy as the sew-
ing machine, for it takes the odd stitches in the
mechanical department that save money.

Let not the inexperienced reader, who hears of
a lathe for the first time, be frightened at this array of terms, or diverted from the use of it by
the recital. In its simple form, as shown in Fig. 1,

Fig. 1.

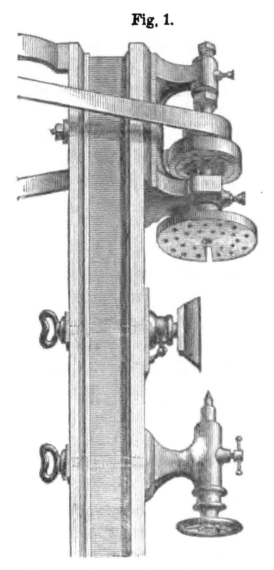

it is readily understood, and, after a little practice, easily managed by any one, and, after the first
few weeks, the amateur will realize the fruits of
his application.

2*

At first, it had not even a continuous rotary motion, but the spindle was driven by a belt worked by a spring pole or its equivalent. The belt was rolled round the spindle, and the pole allowed to spring up; the spindle then revolved the length of the belt, or rope, for belts were not thought of, and the operation was repeated, the work being done only when the force of the spring pole revolved the spindle and the job the right way.

Foot lathes had, prior to the introduction of the engine lathe, been used on very heavy work. It is but a few years, comparatively speaking— not twenty—since cast-iron shafts, six, eight, and ten inches in diameter, were turned in such lathes. For all that we know to the contrary, many jobs, far exceeding this in size, have been thus executed.

In some shops, there are still standing heavy oaken shears, made of timber twenty inches deep, and four or six inches wide, faced with boiler iron, and in the racks above there are long-shanked tools, with which the men of old were wont to do the work.

These lathes are never used now, except for drilling holes, or for apprentices to practice on, but they serve to show what machinists had to do in olden times, when there were no vise benches

Fig. 2.

to sit on and watch the chips curling off the tool, as men do now.

Hand lathes are not in great favor in large machine shops. They are not used, or should not be, for any purpose except drilling, and then they are no longer hand lathes, but horizontal drilling machines. There is no simple work to be done on a hand lathe that could not be performed to better advantage and more cheaply on a machine constructed for the purpose.

Some large machine shops keep a hand lathe going continually, cutting off stud bolts, facing and rounding up nuts, and similar work. This does not seem profitable. A machine to do this work would do more, of a better quality, than hand labor could.

The foot lathe—the terms hand and foot lathe are synonymous—is generally used, at the present time, by small machinists, manufacturers of gas fixtures, amateurs, etc.; men who do not work a lathe constantly, but are called off to braze or solder, or, perhaps, to fit some detail with a file. For these uses the foot lathe is one of the cheapest of tools; for the same person that does the work furnishes the power also, so that a man working on a foot, or hand lathe, as it is often called, ought to have first-class wages. Moreover, a first-rate foot lathe turner is always a good mechanic, for it takes no small degree of dexterity to perform the several jobs with ease, and dispatch, and certainty. To always get hold of the right tool, to use the same properly, so that it will last a reasonable time without being ground or tempered, to rough-turn hollow places with a square edge, to chase a true thread to the right size every time, without making a drunken one, or a slanting one, to make a true thread inside of an oil cup or a box—all these several tasks require good judgment, dexterity, and a steady hand. Of course, where a slide-rest is used, the case is different. We allude, specially, to a cutting tool managed by the hand.

To do all these things, however, it is necessary to have tools, and good ones, or none. It is an old saying, that a bad workman quarrels with his tools, but a good workman has a right to quarrel with bad tools, if he is furnished with them, through chance or design. It is impossible to excute good work with a dull tool, one badly shaped, or unsuited to the purpose, and, therefore, it is important to set out right at the beginning.

There is no tool more efficient in the hands of a good workman, than the diamond point, Fig. 2, here shown. For roughing off a piece of metal, for squaring up the end, for facing a piece held in the chuck, for running out a curve, or rounding up a globe, it is equally well adapted. It may be truly called the turner's friend.

CHAPTER II.

TOOLS.

ANY one who has watched a novice at work on a lathe, must have remarked the difficulty he has in controlling the tool and keeping up the motion of the treadle at the same time. The two operations are difficult to "get the hang of," to use a homely phrase; but once conquered, the work can proceed. The natural tendency is to slack up or stop the motion of the treadle while the tool is engaged, and the tool is, therefore, at one time under the work, at another time above it, at another jumping rankly in, until, finally, the piece goes whirling out of the center or the chuck, and the operator flushes all over at his awkwardness.

This, of course, is remedied by practice; and as this work is written mainly for the information of beginners and amateurs, we hope that experts and those who know all about hand lathes, will excuse allusion to such simple things as holding the tool properly, and kindred matters.

The lathe must be of such a height as the workman finds convenient, so that he is not obliged to stoop much, and, at the same time, low enough to allow the weight of the body to be thrown on the tool when hard work is to be done. The speed of the lathe ought to be very high on the smallest cone, and there should be three speeds, at least, for different work. The object is to regulate the velocity of the work in the lathe, and keep the motion of the treadle uniform, as near as may be, at all times. It distresses a workman greatly, when chasing a fine thread on a small diameter, if he has to tread fast to get up the proper speed, as he does when there are only two speeds. On the contrary, for larger jobs, it is difficult to keep up a rotary motion if the foot moves slowly, as it must in order not to burn the tool by a high velocity on some kinds of work. Foot lathes, in general, are not geared, although some are, and ought to have wider ranges of speed than they do. Where one class of work is done, however, it makes little difference, but for general turning, the speeds should vary.

Another difficulty experienced by beginners is in holding the tool still—*rigidly so.* They allow it to " bob " back and forth against the work, if it runs untrue, so that it is impossible to make a job. The tool must be held hard down, as if it grew to the rest, and never moved, nor receded, until the cut begun is finished.

The "rest" should be of soft, wrought iron, since that material holds a tool with more tenacity; imposing less strain on the arms of the operator. It should be dressed off smooth as often as it gets badly worn, or cut by indentations. Cast iron is not good, and steel is not so good as wrought iron. A special rest should be kept for chasing threads with, since the least obstacle is enough, when running up a fine thread, to divert the chaser and spoil the job, by making a drunken thread. If we now suppose the lathe to be in good order, the centers true and well-turned to a gauge, the rod (if that is the job) between them and properly "dogged," the centers oiled, and the rest at the right height, we shall be all ready to start. The rest should be high enough to bring the point of the tool a little above the center.

To rough off the outside, and make it run true, is the first step, and the tool must, therefore, be

Fig. 3.

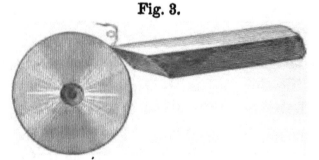

held as in Fig. 3, or so that the point and part of the edge alone engage with the work. This will take off a thin, spiral cut, without springing the shaft or making it untrue. The whole surface of the shaft must be thus run over, beginning at the right hand and shifting the tool as fast as one part is turned. The tool should not be moved rigidly in a straight line toward the belt, but by holding it hard down on the rest, so that the bottom edge bears as in Fig. 2, and rocking the tool on that angle, so that the point describes a curve, as in

Fig. 4.

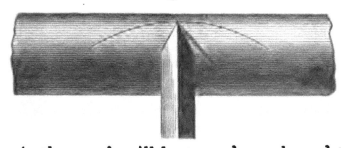

Fig. 4, the work will be turned evenly and true.

We must remark, in passing, that the person who reads these directions, and then undertakes to turn by them, will find that reading how to do a thing, and doing it, are two different matters.

It looks very nice to see a skater darting over the ice at his ease, but try it once, and, if you never knew before, you will understand what experience means. Trying to teach a person to be a turner, in a book, is analogous. One can only indicate the general method, and leave experience to do the rest.

3

After the whole surface has been run over, the same tool may be used on the flat side for reducing the work to one diameter throughout the

Fig. 5.

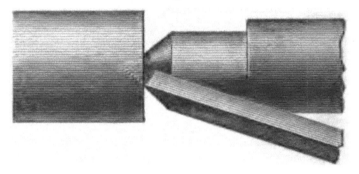

length. The reader must not assume that there is no other tool than a diamond point; he will find many others adverted to, as we proceed.

It is most important that the ends of a rod or shaft should be squared up first, before the body

Fig. 6.

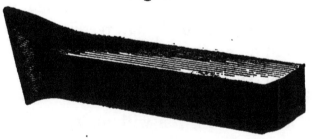

is turned, for the removal of some slight inequality subsequently may cause the whole shaft to run out of truth. The center must be drilled with a

Fig. 7.

small drill, and slightly counter-sunk. When the end is squared up, the center must be run back a little, so that the tool point may project over the drilled hole, and thus make it all true about the center, as in Fig. 5. This will make the work push over to one side of the center, but that is of no consequence. Let it run as it will; so long as it does not come out of the centers there need be no apprehension.

Fig. 6, is another kind of roughing tool, to do heavier work with.

There are two kinds of tools used in foot lathes, called straight and heel tools. Fig. 7 is a heel tool. It is so called from the heel which is forged on the lower end. One form of the straight tool has already been shown. The heel tool is used on heavy work, and the object of it is apparent, namely, to hold on the rest, and so impose but little labor on the workman to retain it in place, or prevent it from receding. It is generally forged from half inch or five eighth steel. The steel is held in a handle twenty inches long, grooved on top to fit the steel, and furnished with a handle at right angles. This handle has a square eye in the top that the tool passes through. A nut at the end of it screws up the eye and binds the tool fast in the groove, so that it cannot slip.

It is given complete in Fig. 7. The lower han-

Fig. 8.

dle enables the workman to have great power over the edge, and to direct it from or to the work without danger of catching. The tool is used by resting the end on the shoulder, as in Fig. 8, and turning the lowest handle. Since the heel holds the tool from slipping, there is no occasion to bear against it. In fact, there is no occasion, at any time, to force the tool from the workman, but it must be turned sideways, back and forth. A piece, properly centered, may be cut in any way without destroying its truth.

3*

CHAPTER III.

SCRAPERS, ETC.

To suit different kinds of work, as previously stated, various tools are needed, but the reader must not expect to see them all illustrated in this book. The workman will learn what tools he needs, and make them for himself, which will be of more advantage to him than engravings could be. The tools here shown, will be found very useful in different places.

Fig. 9.   Fig. 9 is the end of a thin-edged, flat scraper, and is chiefly to be used on brass work. It may be of any length and size, but for small lathes, and light work, it is cheaper and handier to make it of thin sheet steel, one eighth or one tenth of an inch thick, and to form the reverse end into a round nose, or half-circle scraper.

It often happens that fillets or hollows occur, as in finishing ornamental brass work, in connection with flat surfaces. By having such a tool as this, the necessity of laying one tool down and picking up another, is obviated, for the two are combined in one. For iron work, it is customary to use a heavier and thicker tool for finishing. As in Fig.

Fig. 10.

10, the front edge is slightly raised or con-cave, to make it sharp and hold a cut well. All turning tools for finish-ing iron are made thick-er than those for brass, and should have lips, or curved cutting edges. Such tools cannot be used for brass, as they are too sharp; the edges jump into the metal and spoil the work.

A tool for scraping brass work of some kinds is made as shown in Figs. 11 and 12.

Fig. 11.

Fig. 12.

There is no occasion to make the ends at dif-ferent angles, except the convenience, before stated, of having four cutting edges on one piece, for any angle can be easily given by the position of the hand or the direction of the rest. These tools, here alluded to, are only to be used when the job has been all turned true and the scale removed ; they *scrape*, merely, they do not cut.

Such tools sometimes save a few steps at a critical period; that is, when the tool is well set and in place, so that the work is done better and more expeditiously. Apart from this consideration, there is the chance of cutting or injuring the hands, by the proximity of sharp edges. Under the control of an expert, however, there is little danger from this cause, as inspection will show. Skilful men that have worked a lifetime at their trade, have few marks or scars on their hands, as a general thing.

When these scrapers are used on cast iron, or, indeed, on brass of a peculiar composition, they sometimes "chatter," as it is called, and leave the work full of deep, unsightly marks, like those on the edge of coins. The cause of chattering is the rapid vibration of the tool, so that it springs away from, and against the work, with great rapidity, leaving traces of its edge on the work. Chattering may be prevented, by putting a piece of sole leather on the rest, between it and the tool.

The tools with long handles are chiefly intended for heavy work, or that which requires both hands to the cut, but there are smaller tools than these, used by amateurs, wherein the common file handle, or one like it, only a little longer, is employed instead.

CHASING AND SCREW CUTTING.

In an engine, or power lathe, all screws are cut by trains of gears, as mechanics well know, but in the hand lathe, which was the first machine, screws, both male and female, must be made by chasers or hubs, both inside and outside. The chaser itself must be made first, however, and that is done by a simple tool called "a hub."

Fig. 13.

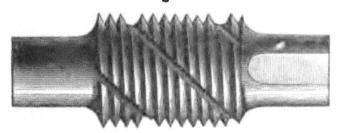

The chaser is first forged in blank, for an out-

Fig. 14.   Fig. 15.

side chaser, as in Fig. 14, and as in Fig. 15 for an

inside tool. It is then filed up, and held against a hub, shown in Fig., 13, running in the lathe. This rapidly cuts away the chaser blank, and forms the teeth in it perfectly. The lines across it are spiral grooves, cut completely round from one side to the other, so that the hub cuts the blank like any other tool. Fig. 16 represents the chaser.

Fig. 16.

CHAPTER IV.

CHASERS, ETC.

IT is not always an easy task to chase a true thread on a piece of work, and even "the boldest holds his breath for a time," if he has a nice piece of work all done but the thread, and that in a critical part. It is so easy to make a drunken thread, or one in which the spirals are not true, but diverge or waver in their path around the shaft, that many are made. That they are more common than true threads, is well known to mechanics. To start a thread true is quite easy with an inside chaser; for, strange as it may seem, it is seldom that a drunken thread is made on inside work; only have the bore itself true, and the chaser will run in properly. The case is different when a bolt or shaft is to be cut. With fine threads, the slightest obstruction on the rest will cause the chaser to catch and stop slightly. No matter how slight the stoppage, it is certain to damage the thread. The injury is more perceptible on fine threads than on coarse, for, in the former, if the threads do not fit (as they will not if they are drunken, one crossing the other, when both parts are put together), the drunken thread will not come fair with the other. In coarse threads, however, it will not be so apparent, for, by making the drunken thread smaller, it will have play and accommodate itself to its place. This is not workmanship, it is "make-shift."

To chase a true thread the rest must be smooth and free from burrs or depressions. Nice workmen keep a special rest, with a hard, polished steel edge, expressly for this purpose.

If the chasers themselves are smoothly finished at the bottom, on an emery wheel, they are all the better. With these precautions, and others noted below, success is certain. When a thread is to be started, take a fine diamond-pointed tool, and hold it on the end of the shaft to be chased. Set the lathe going, and give the tool a quick twist with the wrist, so that a spiral will be traced on the work, like Fig. 17.

Fig. 17.

Some part of this will correspond with the pitch of the thread to be cut, and there is less liability of making it drunken. By a little practice, one is able to hit the pitch of the chaser exactly in making a start.

"There is no trouble, after you once know how." We have chased quantities of small screws, with forty-eight threads to the inch, and not a sixteenth of one inch in diameter. If the chaser once hesitates on such screws, they are spoiled. For heavy threads—seven and eight to the inch, which is about as hard work as any one wants to do,—it is the custom of some turners to use a tool with only two teeth, and some use only a sharp-edged cutter, like Fig. 18, to deepen the

Fig. 18.

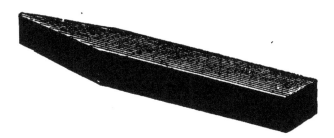

thread, the chaser being used afterward, to rectify the job. There is danger with this tool, unless it is used by an expert, of digging out the thread, so that the last end of it will be worse than the first.

Another tool, used in chasing heavy threads, is a doctor. This consists in having a fac-simile of the thread to be cut on the back of the chaser, and in applying a short set screw behind, so that,

4

as the iron is cut away, the chaser may be followed up behind. Fig. 19 is the doctor, but the follower opposite the chaser is too narrow, and should be made nearly half a circle to avoid slipping; with this exception it is all right.

These tools, and the screws made by them, are all inferior to those made by lathes with traversing mandrels; that is, a mandrel which slides in and out of the head stock, as in a Holtzapffel lathe.

This lathe has a series of hubs, unlike the one shown previously, slipped over the back end of the

Fig. 19.

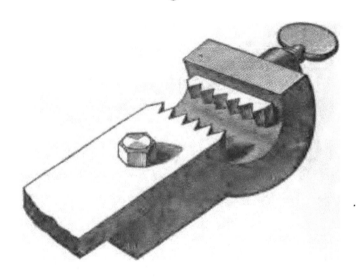

lathe spindle (furthest from the workman) and a fixed nut on the head-stock, which, being put in communication with the hub on the mandrel, drives the same in and out, according to the direction the cone-pulleys are turned. Of course, with such an attachment as this, there is no danger of making drunken threads, for the hubs which start the threads, are cut with a train of gears in an engine lathe, so that it is impossible for them to be incorrect. Moreover, a square thread, or a V-shaped thread, can be made with them, which is not the case with common chasers.

In lathes that have traversing mandrels to cut screws, the tool itself remains stationary, but as this is obviously a disadvantage in many kinds of work, it is far better to have the tool advance and the mandrel revolve as usual. By this plan much time is saved, a greater range of work is possible with the same gear, and a piece that is chucked, or one that is between the centers, can be cut with equal facility.

Any common lathe can be rigged to do this by putting a shell on the back end of the mandrel, between the pulley and the set screw, and slipping the hub over the shell, with a feather, to keep it from turning. To take a thread from this hub, a round bar must be set parallel with the shears, in easy-working guides. The bar must have an arm at one end, to reach over to the hub, said arm to be fitted with a piece of hard wood, to match the thread on the hub. The other end of the bar has the cutting tool in it; of course, at right angles, so as to run in to the work, and bear on the tool rest. The tool is held in an arm on the bar by a set screw, so that it can be lengthened or shortened.

By this arrangement, a true thread can be rapidly generated on any rod, hollow cylinder, or other kind of work—the pitch depending on the pitch of the hub.

It is necessary to have as many different hubs, varying in pitch, as there are different kinds of work to be done, and, although the thread on the hub is only an inch or half an inch long, perhaps, a screw of any length may be cut on a rod, by simply shifting the cutter on the rest. This same bar is also useful for turning, as with a slide rest, for, by sliding it along gradually, it acts, in a measure, like a fixed tool in a slide rest.

Fig. 20.

From these hints the amateur who takes a lathe in hand for the first time, or is, at best, a neophyte, may learn much to his advantage. Persons of a mechanical turn only need a hint, when the mind springs to the conclusion with surprising rapidity.

The little tool, shown in Fig. 20, is very handy in many instances, particularly for running under the necks of screws when the thread is cut up to the head. By so making them, the head comes fair down upon its bed, and holds much better.

4*

CHAPTER V.

CHUCKING.

Chucking work in the lathe is one of the most interesting branches, for here there are no centers in the way, to plague the workman, and the tool has a fair sweep at all parts. Every one who uses a lathe, should get a scroll chuck, Fig. 21, of Cush-

Fig. 21.

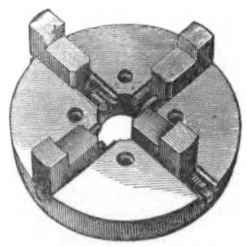

man's make, (A. Cushman, Hartford, Connecticut,) that is, a chuck where the jaws move up together toward the center, so that any round piece will be held perfectly true. This is a great convenience, for whether we have a ring to bore out, or a wheel to turn off, it is equally handy, and is far better than the independent jaw chuck, which has

to be set up by mea- surement, and repeat- ed trials before it is right. To those who cannot afford to pur- chase a scroll chuck, a wooden one can be made to answer eve- ry purpose. Wooden chucks should be made

Fig. 22.

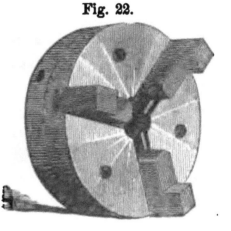

of some hard, fine-grained wood, such as maple or mahogany, so that they will hold well whatever is driven into them.

Fig. 23.

Fig. 24.

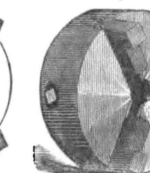

If we have a small cylinder head to turn, for instance, the back head, which has no hole in it to put a mandrel through, as the front one has, the wooden chuck will come in play. To make one, the turner takes a square block of the proper

Fig. 25.

thickness, say one inch, and saws the corners off, so that it is eight-sided. It is then ready to screw on the face plate of the lathe. This is quickly done by having small screw holes in the plate for this purpose, as shown in Fig. 1, page 17.

Fig. 26.

The block is then all ready to work on, and the face must be turned off true, and a recess cut out in it to receive the head. This is the head, Fig. 26.

On the back side, there is a projection to fit the cylinder of the engine. This must be turned first, and the flange faced off true: after that the head must be pryed out, (by making a little recess in the chuck, alongside of it,) reversed, and put in the chuck again, the finished side in, so as to polish it on the outside. Fig. 27. It must be driven up tight against

Fig. 27.

the face of the chuck, otherwise the flange will be thicker on one side than the other. In finishing, it will be found better to commence near the center, and work out toward the largest diameter, for it is necessary to get under the scale, or sand, left on in casting, first, before the work can be turned true, and this is easiest done by beginning at the middle, where the speed is low. The scale is fused sand melted on the metal in the act of casting. The best tool to do this with is the diamond-point, for it can be employed universally on straight or hollow surfaces, is easily ground, and always works well. After it, comes the scraper, previously shown. If these chatter, a piece of leather must be put between them and the rest. It is also well to put a stout iron rod, or piece of hard wood, between the back center of the lathe and the face of the plate; this keeps everything steady, as shown below, so that a beautiful luster will be given by the tool alone.

After the plate or head is firmly scraped, it must be polished with flour emery and oil. The emery first used must be No. 1, which is about like Indian meal; if the work is brass, however, this will not be needed. This must be plentifully supplied with oil, so that it is like cream, and the workman, taking a soft pine stick, with the end pounded into a brush, so that it will hold emery, holds it hard up against the face of the head. If it has been properly scraped, a few revolutions will produce a fine-grained finish, but if it is badly done, the corners will be full of scratches and chatters. It takes time and experience to make a good finisher, and patience also, for men who are good turners, and can make excellent fits, are sometimes botches at polishing.

After emery of the finest possible description has been used, a little rouge powder should be put on a piece of buckskin and applied to the work. This will make a polish equal to gold on brass, and like silver on iron. Instead of these methods many persons burnish their work. The burnisher is sometimes made of steel, of blood-stone, and of agate. Steel is the material generally employed. It is polished as bright as can be on a buff wheel, and must be preserved so, otherwise it is useless to attempt doing anything with it. Pumice stone is very good for polishing with, or rather for finishing the surface before polishing. Other substances will be mentioned hereafter. Steel and iron are best polished with a sharp tool and water. To turn steel with a handsome surface, the tool must be sharpened on an oil stone, and the speed high, then spit on the work and take light cuts, and you will have a nice job. To make a very brilliant polish on steel, it is necessary to use emery and oil, plenty of oil and not much emery, but this makes such a nasty mess on the lathe, that few good turners will do it. A file should not be used in the lathe if possible; filing a job makes it uneven, and spoils the looks of it. It is difficult to avoid scratches, and the expert can generally tell the difference between work that has been turned true, and that which has been filed, and, in nearly all cases, it is quicker to turn the work to fit or to finish at once.

In polishing round work, such as rods or shafts, it is much cleaner, and more expeditious, to make a pair of clamps like Fig. 28, and put the emery and oil on leather pads between them. The clamps consist of two straight pieces of soft or hard wood, lined with leather, though some use sheet lead.

The leather catches the polishing material and holds it, and, at the same time, keeps it continually applied to the shaft. The clamps are slipped over the same, and the ends held in the hand. This utensil also gives a fine finish to the work, making it smooth and even. It must be carried regularly along from end to end, sometimes fast and some, times slow, so as to cross the lines, or avoid making a twist in the polish like a screw thread, which would otherwise be given. A very beautiful and brilliant luster can be given to a shaft of

Fig. 28.

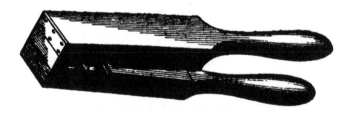

iron or steel, after it is nicely finished, by holding a sheet of fine *sand paper*, covered with chalk, on it. The glaze that this gives, makes the work glisten like silver, but it also takes off all the grease, so that the shaft is very sensitive to moisture, and is quickly rusted.

This discussion about polishing has led us away from the consideration of chucking, which we shall enlarge a little more upon.

The chuck is a very necessary and even indispensable auxiliary when chasing. Threads cannot be caught in the jaws of a scroll chuck, because, if set tight enough to hold the work, the threads are jammed so that they will not run in the part they were fitted to. If a piece, having a thread cut on it, like Fig. 29, is to be turned outside, it is very easy to chase the cap first and then the cup it fits, so that the cap can be screwed into it and turned off where it belongs; it will then be true, and is easy to mill on the edge.

Fig. 29.

It must always be borne in mind that the chaser must be sharp. If it is not, drunken threads will be the rule, not the exception.

The chuck shown in Fig. 30, will be found very useful for holding metallic disks, small box covers, or anything that requires merely a slight clasp; it is also useful for holding round plugs, pencils of wood, or penholders, to drill in the ends. It can be made eccentric with the mandrel of the lathe, if desired, so as to turn a piece on one side, or drill in a similar manner in the end of a plug. It is merely a piece of box-wood bored out, bored with holes, which are sawed down into slots, so as to form a series of

5

jaws, which are sprung in by sliding the ring

Fig. 30.

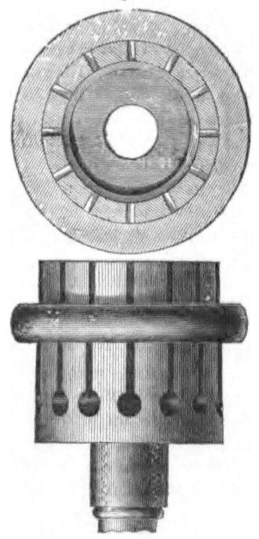

down on them. They are so easily made that a
great many can be provided.

CHAPTER VI.

METAL SPINNING.

SPINNING sheet metal into various forms is another kind of work which can be done in the foot lathe, and it is here that the amateur can show his taste and dexterity.

The process consists in forming a blank, like this engraving, into an ornamental base for a lamp, or an oil cup;
in fact, any thing whatsoever.
All that is requisite is to have a
fac simile, in wood, of the shape
you wish to make. This is bolt-
ed or otherwise made fast to the
face plate, and the blank is then set up against it,
and held as the cylinder head, shown in Fig. 26,
is, that is, with a rod leading from the back center of the lathe to the work.

Fig. 81.

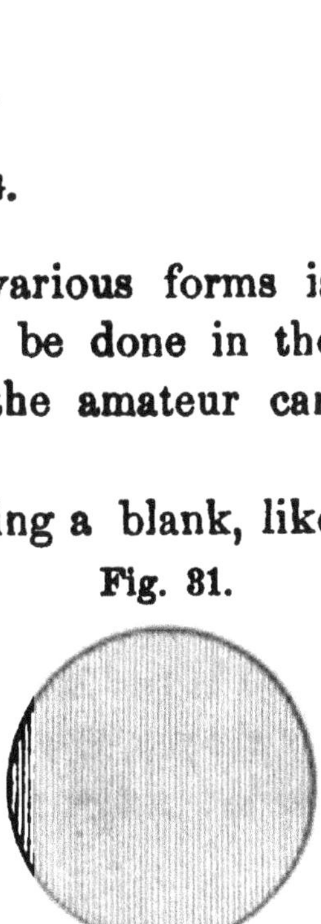

A tool like Fig. 32 is then used to press the metal into all the recesses or curves of the pat-
tern. The speed must be high, and the metal quite soft and moistened with a little soap-suds or oil, so that it will not be scratched by the tool.

To spin metal requires some dexterity, but it is easily acquired after a little practice. The rest must be furnished with holes, like Fig. 33, and a

Fig. 32.   Fig. 33.

pin, so that the tool can be brought up against it like a lever.

Still another kind of metal spinning can be done in the lathe. This relates to making circular shapes, or cylindrical, more properly—such as napkin rings, the tops of steam pipes, or similar

Fig. 34.

things. To do this, a mandrel is requisite. The mandrel must be of steel, and turned to the desired pattern—like Fig. 34, for instance.

A ferrule is then made and soldered together

with lapped edges, so that there will be no seam.
The mandrel must be as much smaller than the
size of the finished work as will allow it to come
off freely, for it will be apparent that if the work
was spun up *on* the mandrel, it could never be
taken off.. The ferrule, when put on them, will
stand eccentric to the mandrel, as
in this figure—that is, when the
tool bears on it. In other respects the process is just the
same as spinning on the face
plate. Tripoli, chalk, whiting,
rotten-stone, and similar sub-
stances are used to give the fine polish on such
work.

Fig. 35.

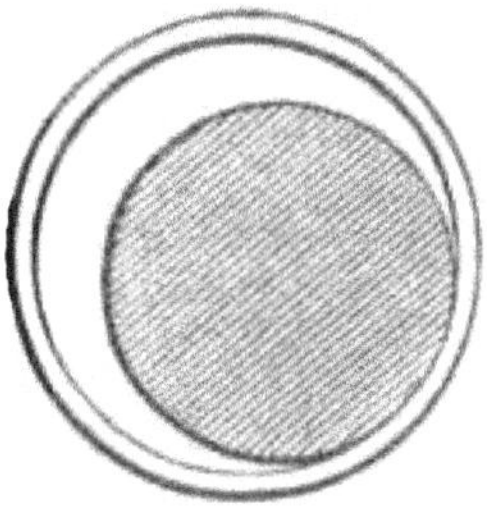

We know of no prettier or more expeditious
process of making a small steam boiler for a toy
engine, than by spinning it upon the lathe. The
boiler will be very strong, have large fire surface,
and be without joints, having only one at the bottom, where it is easily kept tight. Fig. 36 is the
boiler.

The metal must be thin (twenty gauge), the
sheet brass sold in the shops will answer, as it is
already annealed, and the corrugations must not
be too deep on the sides, or the work will not
come off the mould. The center of the fire-box,
A, must be left flat, so that the flue will have a

5*

bearing on it. For a small engine, 1-inch bore, and 2-inch stroke, a boiler of the dimensions given here is ample. The flue must be brazed or soldered at A, and the bottom must be riveted at B, for every two inches; this is not necessary, however. There are only three pieces in this boiler—the shell, the fire-box, and the flue, and the water must not be carried more than three-fourths of an inch over the crown of the furnace.

We shall now again revert to cutting tools.

Fig. 36.

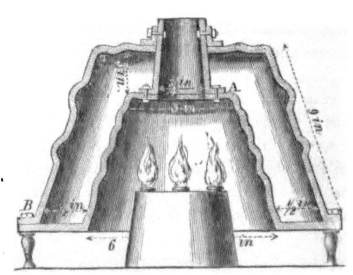

Probably many of our readers, who use hand lathes not furnished with slide rests, have wished for that indispensable appendage where boring is to be done. For ordinary turning, we do not appreciate a slide rest on a hand lathe so much as many do that we know, but for boring out valves, cocks, or, in fact, anything, a scroll chuck and a good slide rest are invaluable.

Some persons are always "meaning" to do a thing, yet never do it. Sometimes, for the want of facilities, at others for the lack of an idea. If the latter be of any value, we can furnish one or two on this subject that may be useful.

One way to bore out holes parallel, without a slide rest, is to do it with the spindle of the back head. With a tool of peculiar construction, holes varying in size, can be bored beautifully in this way. We present a view of such a tool in Fig.

Fig. 37.

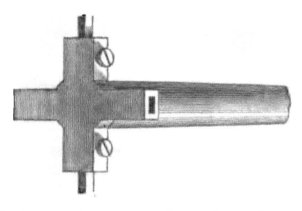

37. It is merely a cross, formed on the end of a center fitting the back spindle, the same as the lathe center does. The arms of the cross are made stout and thick, so as to admit of a square hole being cut in them. The hole is made by

drilling in and driving in a square drift afterwards
to take off the corners. The shanks of the tools
are well fitted to these holes in the arms, so that
a slight pressure of the screws in the sides of the
arm will hold them steady. When used, the tool
is put in the back spindle, and the cutters set to
the size required, or less, if there is much to take
out, and run through the work in an obvious manner. Any range of size can be had up to the diameter of the cross. It is not well to run the
cutters out too far, however, as they will jump and
chatter, or spring, and make bad work. The tool

Fig. 38.

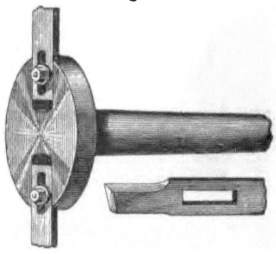

is so easily made that one can afford to have three
or four, for different jobs.

Another plan, but not so good, is to make a
common center and disk, like Fig. 38.

Here the cutters have a slot in them, through which a bolt passes and screws into the disk; a small piece of wood put at the bottom of the tool, between it and the cutter, prevents it from slacking off so as to diminish the cut. These tools will be found useful, and will do good work if properly handled. This latter tool is better for wood, but will answer for any metal by varying the cuttter.

To make a slide rest, in the common way, is a costly and tedious job. For all purposes of boring, a good one may be made as shown in the following engraving, Fig. 39.

Fig. 39.

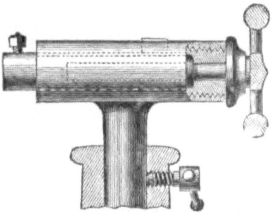

This is simply a casting fitted with a screw and spindle, as shown. The spindle has a tool let in the front end and held there by a set screw, and there is a wheel at the back end to run the spindle in and out. The casting has a leg to it which enables it to fit the common post the rest for the hand tool fits. There is also a key to prevent the spindle from turning round. By this arrangement it is easy to bore, not only parallel holes of any size, but tapering ones, which is often a great convenience. By a simple change of tool, it can also face off any casting, and can easily be made to cut a thread, of a given pitch, by any ingenious workman. Not only this, but it can also be made without planing; or other work most amateurs have no facilities for. It is within the range of ordinary lathe work, and will be found indispensable. The T-head may be of cast iron, but the spindle should be steel, with a brass nut let in the back end for the screw to work in.

CHAPTER VII.

ORNAMENTAL CUTTING.

I SHALL now give some examples of turning different things which are useful and interesting to
work. These are only hints, and I make no claim
to discovery, or to anything specially novel or
ingenious. It would be very foolish to do that,
for what seems remarkably "cute" to the de-
signer of any particular thing, is often shown to
be slow and unmechanical, compared to other
ways by other men. I hope, therefore, that the
expert will bear in mind the fact that, while he
may know better ways to do the same thing, beginners are glad to receive instruction first, and
improve upon it, so much as they are able, after.

TO MAKE A PAIR OF SOLITAIRE SLEEVE BUTTONS.
—*Solitaire* buttons are those which have so lately
come in fashion; that is, a single stud with two
eyes on the back for the button-holes of the
wristband. It is easier to make one stud on the
back of the button, and easier to fasten it to the
shirt, as that is the kind I shall describe.

Go to any dealer in box-wood, and procure

·waste stuff, which he will sell at a small price. Take a piece an inch square, put it in the chuck, and turn it round on one end as far as you can, then reverse it, and turn the other end ; this will make a round plug. Take a ten-cent piece, and

Fig. 40.

Fig. 41.

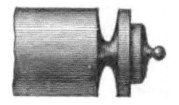

chuck it, either in a wooden or scroll chuck. Cut out the center, so that you have a silver ring. It will be necessary to have two rings, one for each button. Put the box-wood in the lathe and turn the end as in Fig. 41. On the shoulder you are to shrink the silver ring just made, Fig. 40. To

Fig. 42.

fasten the ring properly, you have only to leave the center part of the box-wood a little larger than the silver ring—say the thickness of a sheet of paper —heat the ring slightly on a stove or over a spirit lamp, and clap it on to its place. When it is cool, if properly done, no power can remove it without destroying the button. When the ring is in place, it only remains to turn it off as ornamentally as the workman desires. The edge may be milled, and

Fig. 43.

the face chased or left smooth. The center of the button, which is of wood, may be drilled in, and

6

a square ebony plug put in, which will give it a unique appearance, as shown in Fig. 42. In like manner ivory buttons may be turned and breast-pins spun up, either in gold or silver. Brass breastpins may be ornately turned, and afterwards electro-plated for a trifle. They will thus be cheaply made, and the ingenious turner can please his lady friends by presenting them with speci-mens of his dexterity and taste.

At the commencement of this book, I alluded to lathes with traversing mandrels, and to varieties of work done by tools not generally employed— that is, those which are not used by the hand, but in connection with the lathe, and driven by belt-ing from a counter shaft over head. I give an illustration of such a tool, in one form, in Fig. 43, It may be screwed in the tool post of the slide

Fig. 44.

rest, or otherwise at-tached to the lathe, and the belt from the counter shaft carried over the small pulley. The driving pulley over head should be very large, so as to give a great velocity to the cutter, at least fifteen hundred revolutions per minute. The use of this tool is to make ornamental designs—circular carving, it might be called—on all kinds of turned work, as, for instance, in Fig. 44, where a small box for pins or needles is shown. This box is made by putting a piece of hard, fine-grained wood in the chuck, boring the hole and cutting the thread. It is then removed, driven on a round mandrel held in the chuck, turned off round outside, and then prepared for the pattern as follows:—The design settled upon, the index plate must be brought into use, and the points inserted in such holes as will bring the pattern out right, or all the spaces equal —just as the teeth of gears are cut. The tool shown in Fig. 43, may be any desired shape. In the example of work, Fig. 44, it is made half round, and the pattern is called "bamboo," from a resemblance to wickerwork. The pattern is made to break joint, as mechanics say, that is, it alternates, so that the commencement of one part meets in the middle of the other. After one course is made all the way round, the tool is shifted on to another course, and the index changed as above mentioned, until the whole has been gone over. This produces a beautiful effect.

It is easy to see that a change of pattern is produced at will, by altering the kind of tool and the index. As, for instance, in Fig. 45, where the pattern is entirely straight. When the design is to be cut on such work, it is extremely convenient to have a pair of centers to set on the lathe, across the bed; then the flying tool is not needed, nor the index on the lathe pulleys either, that on the centers being used instead. When this box is held between the centers so as not to mar it, the handle may be turned and the work run along under the cutter, with great facility. The grooves shown in the box are first drilled at each end with a common drill, just to the corner of the drill, so that a neat and handsome finish is given; a V-shaped cutter is then put in a mandrel

Fig. 45.

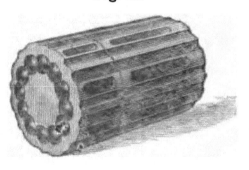

between the centers of the lathe, and the pulleys set going, so that when the work is run under the tool, the slot or groove will be formed. The circlet, at the top of the box, is made by a crescent drill ground very thin and made sharp—a drill like a fish's tail, only formed on a half circle.

Of course, these methods of doing this kind of work can, as I have said before, be varied infinitely, and are only cited as applicable to a common foot lathe.

CHAPTER VIII.

CENTERS.

An indispensable article on a foot lathe, where any fancy work is to be done, is the centers—of which I have before spoken—shown in Fig. 46. These consist of a common set of heads, with spindles fitted to them. One spindle has an index plate and spring, and the other has a common center. These heads set on a slide that is moved back and forth over a rest, screwed to the lathe bed as usual. It is easy to see that, with this, we can do some very fine cabinet work. Suppose we have a round vase turned up handsomely, and wish to flute the base or make it a series of curves all round; to do this, we have only to put it in the centers, set the index so as to come out even, as before explained, and go ahead.

The kind of cutter to be used is a sort of gouge, set in a cast-iron head, something as a plane iron is set in its stock. That is, fitted tight to a groove and held by a set screw. Two of these cutters should be used, at equal distances apart, and the cutter head should be keyed on a short shaft, set

6*

between the main centers of the lathe.   The

Fig. 46.

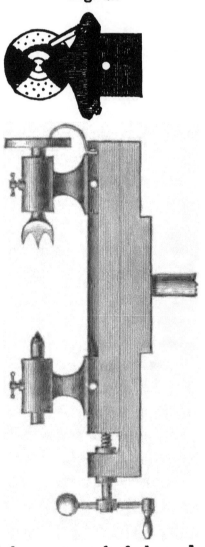

whole should be accurately balanced, or else the work will be full of chatters or ridges.   Since centrifugal force increases as the square of the velocity, any thing that runs a little out of truth, will be very much exaggerated as the speed increases. By using cutters of different shapes, beautiful effects can be produced; as, for instance, suppose we take a common round-nose cutter, set the index so as to divide the circle of the job we are to work on in twenty-four parts, and execute

Fig. 47.

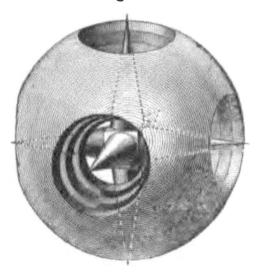

that part of the design, then take a tool forming an ogee, and work out the spaces intervening, we shall find that the article, when completed, will have a beautiful appearance, and that, instead of being round, the bottom will be octagonal, which will present a pleasing contrast to the rest.

The centers can be set at any angle with the cutter shaft and a pineapple pattern can be made

on straight surfaces, by executing one part at one
angle, then reversing the rest that carries the
centers, and finish the remainder, one part of the
pattern crossing the other.

I present here views of a novel ornament which
exhibits great mechanical ingenuity and manual
dexterity, but is otherwise of no value. It consists, in one form, of a globe with a series of rings
or globes inside, and a six-armed spur projecting
through holes—all cut out of one solid piece. Fig.
47

Fig. 48.

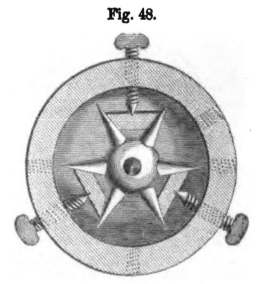

Fig. 48 shows how the points are turned. After
the internal rings are cut out with a quadrant tool
like Fig. 49, and the spur also severed, by cutting
in the ends o' the holes (not boring them out

solid), th globe is put in a shell chuck, with three set screws in it, as shown. The set screws go through the holes in the globe, and the cross

Fig. 49

pieces, in between the spurs, serve to steady the job. Any number of points may be turned in the globe. Fig. 50 shows a polygon with many

Fig. 50.

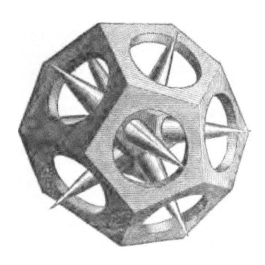

spurs turned inside. At first sight it would appear that the tool, severing the rings, would cut off the points also, but it will be seen that this is not the case, for the holes being bored so as to leave a core standing (which afterward serves to make the points of the spur), the severing tool falls into the holes and goes no further, and each division serves as a guide for the tool in the next hole, so that the globe is made the same size, without jags. The quadrant tool, shown before, must be followed round the shell in the act of cutting it out, so that it will make the same round, and the globe must be shifted in the chuck, to reach all the holes. It is no easy task to make this little affair, for all it looks so simple.

CHAPTER IX.

FANCY TURNING.

FIG. 51 is another, a little more ornate and of a different pattern. The process is essentially the same, except that there are no spurs and a solid disk is left inside. This disk is turned out of a

Fig. 51.

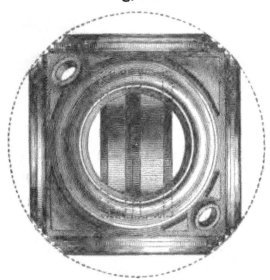

ball, left inside the exterior shell. One side of it is squared up before the ball is cut free from the globe, and the job is then reversed and the other side squared. The ball is then cut free, and the loose disk is held fast between a flat-ended driver in the live spindle, and a loose, flat-ended button on the back center. The diameter is then decided through the hole which is toward the reader.

A little tool, which is very convenient for mak-

Fig. 52.

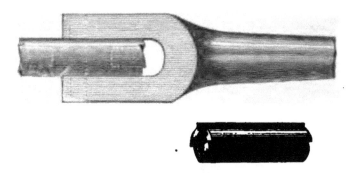

ing small screws, is here shown in Fig 52, rather out of place, but it was overlooked before. In construction it explains itself. Holes of different sizes are made in a steel rod, and the end filed into shape, as seen. It has been found difficult by some to make these cutters work, but that was because they were not properly made. The trouble lies in drilling the hole. When the drill starts at first, the hole is larger on the outside, so that the screw blank, when cut, gets tighter as it goes in, and twists it off.

The remedy is, to drill the hole in some distance and then turn off the outside end, so that it gets where the bore is the same size. This refers only to small bolts, a sixteenth of an inch in diameter; where they are large, the trouble mentioned is not experienced.

It is convenient to have two sizes in the tool so that the heaviest part of the work can be done by one cutter, the tool reversed by turning it over in the fork of the jaws, and finishing the blank with the last cutter. A watchmaker's fine saw is to be used to sever the screw from the rod. The tool itself is to fit in the spindle of the tail stock, and the screw wire is held by a drill chuck.

In the matter of ornamental work, there are other details and plans in vogue among experienced turners, which can only be alluded to, not discussed at length, for the reason that the styles are so numerous that an elaborate work might be made of them alone, with great profit. The scroll chuck or geometrical chuck, as it is sometimes called, is a complicated piece of mechanism, too costly for general use, and too limited in its application, to mechanics in general, to be of much utility. It does such work as may be seen on bank bills. The chuck plate, on which the work is fixed, is connected, by a train of gearing on its back, with a fixed gear about the spindle on the head stock, so that when the relation these gears bear to one another is altered, the motion of the work on the chuck is accelerated or retarded, or

7

is made to assume certain positions. An elliptic chuck is quite another thing, the work done by it is shown in Fig. 53, which consists, chiefly, of ornamental designs disposed in a certain order. In fact, the changes that can be made are infinite.

Fig. 53.

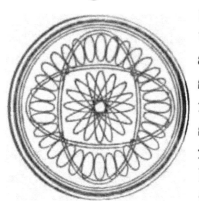

Mandrels—arbors, as many call them—are very useful tools. Mandrels are made of wood and steel—usually steel, and never of wood, unless for some special reason. As, for instance, when a large brass ring has to be turned. For this use a wooden mandrel is cheaper and more quickly made than a steel one. Besides, it is quite as good. Wooden mandrels should have iron center plates let in them, so that they will run true; if the center was made in the wood itself, it would be liable to run out. Take a piece of sheet iron, one eighth of an inch thick and one inch square, hammer the corners thin, then turn them over at right angles with the plate. This gives four sharp corners, so that, when driven in the end of a block, it will not slip; three small screws will hold the plate to the mandrel so that it cannot get loose. The center must then be countersunk, as any other is. Such a mandrel, made of hard wood, hickory for instance, will last a long time.

Fibrous wood such as white oak, makes a good mandrel, for the reason that work, driven on it, compresses the fibers instead of scraping them, so that the size of the mandrel is unchanged,

Steel mandrels should be turned two in one, or largest in the middle, for small work, each end being a different size. Each end should be thoroughly centered with a drill, and countersunk, and a flat place filed so that the dog will hold; not a scratch with a tool should ever be made in one, though few persons will take the pains to avoid doing this.

It is unnecessary to tell the mechanic he must have a rack for his tools, but we may tell the beginner so, and he will find it a great convenience.

Now-a-days, the twist drills, made and sold in all the tool stores, are so uniformly superior to any thing that can be made by hand, or by individuals, and are, moreover, so cheap, that it is foolish to make drills. Those who have never used them, should not fail to order sets. They run all sizes, from a needle to an inch.

There are not a few turners who spoil work simply from heedlessness. Not because they do not know any better, but because they are averse to taking a little extra pains. If a mandrel runs out of truth a very little, sooner than alter it, or make a new one, they will try to " make it do." The result is easily seen when work is to be put together. Moreover, many persons use little caution in setting their work in the lathe. Instead of always putting it in the same place, driving it from the same side of the face plate, it is entered at hap-hazard. It is not good to get into the habit of doing work in this way, for it soon leads to recklessness.

Some are too lazy to go and grind their tools, when they know it should be done, and continue to use them to the ultimate damage of the work. It is easy for the practiced eye to see these apparently small things, for they constitute a great part of the difference between a good workman and a bad one.

CHAPTER X.

ORNAMENTAL WOODS.

In the matter of wood working, the amateur has a field as wide and attractive as the most enthusiastic could wish. Of course, under this head only those that are ornamental are considered, leaving the plainer and rougher materials for domestic purposes.

VARIETIES.

Most amateurs ransack the stores of dealers in foreign woods, for rich and rare varieties, leaving our own native woods for others, of deeper hue and harder grain. Yet it would be difficult to find more beautifully veined wood than chestnut, butternut, some varieties of ash, the root of the black walnut, California rosewood, and oak; all of which are indigenous.

In foreign woods there are innumerable varieties, but as comparatively few of them are to be had, there can be nothing gained to the amateur by mere enumeration. I have said comparatively few are to be had in shops, and that is true for

7*

this reason; the woods the amateur can readily obtain, are the woods of commerce; that is, those used in the arts and trades. No one imports woods at a venture, or on chance of sale. Dealers know their customers, and when, by chance, they find a captain of some foreign. trader, who has a fancy lot which he has brought over, they send word to their best buyers, who come and view the lot, and take that which suits them, and the rest, worm-eaten and " wind-shaken," it may be, is either burnt up, or thrown on one side for some button maker, who may find in the short odds and ends a profitable bargain. I shall, therefore, mention but a few of the leading varieties of choice woods, and these the most marked and contrasted. Very many differ only in the name, and, as far as mere exterior goes, are hardly distinguishable from each other, while others are positively ugly.

SNAKE WOOD.

Prominent on the list of foreign woods is snake wood, or, as it is sometimes called, leopard wood. The markings and mottlings in this wood are certainly superb in fine specimens. I have now before me a small vase, made of this material, which exhibits the most beautiful cloudings and veinings. The pattern, so to speak, is in alternate black and red blotches, like those on the back of a snake. When varnished and French polished, these are brought out in strong relief, and the effect is very fine. There is one drawback to its use, however, and that is its brittleness. Notwithstanding the lathe be run at a high speed, it will frequently sliver and crack in the most unlooked-for and vexatious manner, and it is unsafe to undertake any very delicate or fine work that requires time and minute separation on the surface in this material; for general work, however, which has mouldings and convolutions on it, it is easily manipulated, and is susceptible of a brilliant polish. Further: it has the advantage of being "fast colors," which is more than can be said of many other foreign woods. Whatever color may be developed in turning, will be retained to the end of time. This is not true of either tulip or granadilla wood. Both of these are brilliant in the extreme, when freshly cut, but by exposure to the air, fade away into the most sombre colors.

TULIP WOOD.

This is a moderately hard wood, of a peculiar salmon-pink, veined with reddish brown and gray. The veinings are chiefly parallel with the grain, not straight, of course, but wavy and mottled. As previously remarked, it is beautiful when first cut, but gradually fades into a dingy, reddish brown. It is a handsome wood for contrasting with ebony, or any dark variety, and is chiefly used for inlaying costly furniture, such as musical instruments, work boxes, etc., etc. It is undeniably handsome, however, and by no means to be disparaged.

GRANADILLA.

This is commonly called cocoa wood. It is hard, finely-veined, and capable of a handsome polish. It is largely used in the manufacture of table and pocket cutlery, for the handles. It comes in logs, from two to eight inches in diameter, and is one of the most easily worked woods. Quantities of it are employed for the handles of seals or letter stamps, in which instruments its brownish yellow color and markings must be familiar to many. It fades, however, so that in time it becomes almost uniform in its tone.

TAMARIND.

This wood is very unfrequently met with. I obtained, by chance, a large log of a wood-worker, and was highly pleased with it. It can scarcely be called variegated, except so finely as to be unnoticeable, but for a rich brown color and tint it is unapproachable. It is chocolate brown in hue, and so hard and close in fibre, as to rive like the husk of a cocoanut, while under a burnisher alone it polishes like ivory. It is seldom one meets with a wood so wholly satisfactory, in its general nature, for all kinds of work where a hard grain and fine surface is desirable.

CAM WOOD.

This is a dye wood; that is, the shavings boiled in water, or treated with alcohol, yield a handsome dye, which is largely used in the arts. It is moderately hard, in about the same degree as mahogany, and is plain in surface; it is handsome for inlaying and veneering in contrast with ebony, but changes to a brown with age.

BOX WOOD.

This is so well known to be a fine-grained, buff yellow color, and easily worked wood, as to need little further explanation of its characteristics. It is becoming scarcer and dearer every year, but is of little general value to the amateur from its monotonous sameness; one piece being like all the others; whereas, with snake wood, or granadilla, perpetual surprises await one. Refuse box wood, in odd-shaped pieces, can be bought very cheap from those who make it a business to fit up blocks for engravers, and also from wood-type makers.

LAUREL ROOT.

This is a peculiar wood, and, in my opinion, more peculiar than pretty. It has a singular feeling under the tool, cutting much like cheese or gum ; like any thing else, in fact, but wood. In veining, it closely resembles brier wood and bird's eye maple; pipes have been made of it. It is quite sound, but cannot be said to be handsome. It is the root of the common swamp laurel, I am told, and requires long seasoning and drying to be manipulated.

WHITE HOLLY.

This is a pure white wood, very easily bent, turned, and cut, straight of grain, and very useful for inlaying. Quantities of needle cases, fans, and such wares, are made of it. It is a native of this country, though the best is said to come from England. This seems quite unnecessary, for I have picked out of my wood-pile quantities of white holly, as handsome in color and in grain, as one could wish to see.

EBONY.

Every one has his prejudice, and I have no doubt but that many will consider me lacking in taste if I condemn this wood. It has one sole re-deeming feature—blackness—which renders it indispensable in many cases. Yet I have seen rock maple dyed black, that put ebony to shame for richness of color and fineness of grain. No ebony that I ever saw was *black*, naturally. It was brown, and became black by oiling and varnish- ing. There is a variety, called "bastard ebony," which is full of whitish brown stripes, and is soft like pine, but the true ebony is not to me a pre- cious wood, although it is expensive, and, in some cases, undeniably handsome. In spite of all se- lection, aided by good judges, I have frequently found my "black ebony" any thing but black; it is full of season streaks and cracks, and splits in the most perverse and unexpected manner.

OLIVE WOOD.

This is the wood of the olive tree, and is chiefly valuable for its odor; that is, to those who like that odor. In color it is like white wood, and is without any marked feature, except that of scent.

SANDAL WOOD.

This is a fragrant wood, light buff-colored, and very soft, and straight in grain. In general it is like pine wood, splitting straight, working easily, and valuable solely for its odor.

ROSE WOOD.

This is an exceedingly beautiful wood, and is so well known, in its general nature, as to need no recommendation. In marking, it is so delicate as to admit of the finest work, and yet retain the beauty of the pattern.

CURLED MAPLE.

This is one of the most beautiful of our native woods; in point of color, and power of retaining it, in marking and in variety, it is, to me, one of the most beautiful of all woods. The vein has a sinuous sweep and curve to it, which is heightened by varnishing and polishing, to a marked degree. All of the handsome woods, however, have a peculiar intractability, so to speak, which renders them slow and tedious to work. In fact, it is just this stubbornness of grain which renders them beautiful, for, by running in all directions, interlacing the fibres, so that the end of the grain is alternately presented side by side with the parallel grain, the light is caught and retained on dead surfaces that absorb it, making those beautiful contrasts which the most uncultivated admire.

BIRD'S EYE MAPLE.

This is also a handsome wood, full of round spots interspersed with circular markings, the whole forming a handsome contrast when well handled. Pear and apple tree woods are also handsome, but none of the native woods exhibit so great variety in tint and markings, as those which grow in tropical countries. There is no occasion to continue a mere list of woods which can be found in any shop, and this branch of the subject will be dropped.

TREATMENT.

The first thing that occurs to the workman when he possesses or sees a handsome piece of wood, is: What shall I make with it? Many kinds of wood show well in large works, but in smaller wares, such as sleeve buttons, and napkin rings, they look like common wood; it is, therefore, labor lost to spend time in working out a nice job to show the veining and marking of the wood, because such veining is not brought out fully. The first care is to select sound wood. It is one of the most vexatious things in the world to have a nice job nearly done, and find a large worm hole extending right through the center of it, interfering with the tool and destroying the beauty of the piece. In such a case, the only resort is to plug it up, but no matter how skillfully this is done, the plug is certain to show, and always mars the appearance. Some kinds of

8

foreign woods are almost always worm eaten. Snake wood, for instance, is very liable to that fault, and too much care cannot be taken in examining it. Ebony is not so liable to it, and native woods are peculiarly free from it.

CHAPTER XI.

WOOD TURNING.

IN turning wood, the speed cannot be too high, or the tool too sharp. The faster the speed, the more perfect the surface produced by the tool. In centering, also, it is necessary to use care in getting a sound place to begin on; otherwise, when in the middle of a job, the centers change and the work is spoiled. This, of course, relates to work that is turned on centers, such as chess-men, pen-holders, rulers with ornamental ends, " what-not " legs ; in fact, anything of that class. The driving center or one that goes in the head of the lathe, commonly called the live center—in opposition to the one in the back end of the lathe head, which does not move, and is called the dead center— should be properly made, or much confusion will be the result. Very many use the common bit, like Fig. 54, which is a very poor device for the purpose. There being no guard at the corners of the bit, they are liable to slip when strain is brought on the work

Fig. 54.

by the tool; it is, therefore, necessary to make the driving bit, or center, like Fig. 55, which represents a section through the front edge and the flat pieces at the top, to prevent the work from slipping.

In turning very small work, say penholders

Fig. 55.

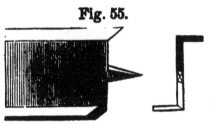

for example, I have found centers useless to drive from, and after trying dogs, commonly used for metal turning, and many other devices, have found no more efficient or expeditious plan than to round the end of the wood slightly with a pocket-knife, as in Fig. 56; insert the rounded end in a chuck, and place the other in the back center. In this way, I am able to command the whole range of the work,

Fig. 56.

from end to end, without interference, and to have the small tip where it is necessary to have it to keep steady; that is, near the center.

I *saw* all my pieces for turning, into square strips. I never split them; splitting shivers and cracks hard and precious wood, and makes unsound that which was previously sound.

Besides, it is more economical and more expeditious. If you cannot saw them yourself,
handily, take them to the nearest wood-worker -
who has a circular saw, and he will do it for a
trifle.

8*

CHAPTER XII.

TOOLS FOR WOOD TURNING.

IT does not seem necessary to go into the discussion of tools, or shapes of tools, for wood turning, for the grand and great reliance for roughing is the gouge, and a skillful workman will do as many things with it as the Russian carpenter is said to do with his axe, which is almost his only tool. For smoothing, there is the flat chisel, and for special work, every one will find tools, or, rather, make those he finds best suited to his needs.

I would, however, here say with great earnestness, that it makes all the difference in the world what kind of steel you get in your tools, whether they are worth any thing or not. I never found *any* turning tools in stores, that I considered worth any thing. They are generally made for working soft woods, such as pine, but the amateur needs tools of a different class and temper. Hard woods are full of dust on the outside, and seem more or less impregnated with silica, the principle which forms the coating on the stalks of rye and cereal grains generally, which destroys the cutting edge in a short time, and also draws the temper. I have therefore found it convenient to make my own tools out of the best steel I could buy, and temper them myself. The difference is very marked, for where I formerly went to the grindstone every few minutes, I now use a tool a long while, thus saving many steps and minutes.

I therefore repeat—choose your steel from such as you find the best, and harden it yourself. If you don't know how, a few trials will enable you to do it "everytime," as the saying is. I have found Sanderson's, Jessops, and Stubbs, all good steel; also Park Brothers American steel first-rate for general work. No doubt there are some who will take up this book, and for the first time read of the matters contained therein, to whom hardening and tempering are "all Greek;" to such I will explain the process.

Very often amateurs buy tools which are good if they were only properly hardened, and to them also, it may be of service—if they do not already know it—to be able to do this simple thing.

CHAPTER XIII.

TOOL TEMPERING, ETC.

THE great object is to harden at as low a heat as possible, so as not to injure the steel. The tool must not be treated as a blacksmith does iron, nothing like so hot, but so as to be of a dull cherry color. Steel that will not harden at this heat is poor stock. When so heated, plunge it into cold water. This will make the tool hard and brittle, like glass, so that it is not fit to cut with; you must then rub it bright on a piece of emery paper or a grindstone, and hold it in the fire for a second or so at a time, until the temper is drawn to the right degree of toughness and tenacity. This will be, for turning-tools for *hard* wood, of a dull blue-brown, say violet, color. Straw brown is hard enough to cut steel, and you do not want such a temper for wood in general, but for some purposes, it is desirable to have a very hard tool. When the edge *crumbles*, it is too hard, and must be lowered in temper; when it rounds over, or dulls quickly, it is too soft, and needs to be hardened. This much in the way of tools of which more will be said hereafter.

Many things are not held in the centers at all, but are grasped by chucks, of different patterns or shapes. This, to me, is the most satisfactory way of turning, inasmuch as it allows perfect liberty and sweep in all directions, and does not restrict the fancy or imagination of the workman.

It is not necessary to mention *what* kinds of work can be done, for that will occur to every one, but I will merely give here an illustration of the fa-

Fig. 57.   Fig. 58.

cility which the chuck affords for all kinds of work. Fig. 57 is a box cover, and being held at first by the corners, permits the inside to be turned out to fit the bottom. Afterwards, what-ever finish or pattern is desired, can be given to the top. There is in every lathe, a center screw, like Fig. 58, which is useful for holding work that has, or is to have, a hole in it, but for fine work it is not suitable, for the obvious reason that the screw spoils it. Fig. 57 is the scroll chuck, and is a favorite instrument of mine. I could dispense with many things—the face-plate of the lathe for one—better than I could with this. If I want to make a sleeve-button, there is my friend, the scroll chuck, ready to hold the piece true to the center, without any adjustment whatever and hold it firmly, too. If I wish to bore out a ring, the chuck will grasp true, and hold it without spring : in fact, not to dilate unnecessarily, I call it the one thing no turner can afford to be without. There are many in the market, but the best one for general work of this class, I have found to be that made by A. F. Cushman, of Hartford, Connecticut. He makes a very small chuck, also, for holding drills, that is exceedingly convenient for them, and for holding screw wire, or any work of that class. The " Beach Chuck," made by the Morse Twist Drill Company of New Bedford, Massachusetts, is also a good chuck, but as I am not now discussing the merits of chucks, I will return to the subject in hand—treatment of woods.

I do not design, in this little work, telling any one how to hold a tool, for it is to be presumed that at least that part of the craft has been ac-

quired.   Even if I did essay to tell them, I could
no more impart such knowledge than one could
skate by seeing another person do it.   Observa-
tion and practice are the only teachers.

CHAPTER XIV.

ARTISTIC WOOD TURNING.

SOME of the most beautiful work, really artistic in every sense of the word, is made by laying up woods of different colors, *but of the same general character as regards hardness.* If this latter precaution, which I have italicised, be neglected, the result will be wholly unsatisfactory, for where two or more woods of different densities are laid up together, side by side, the tool will act upon the hardest very well, but will glide or spring over the inferior material, and thus leave an uneven surface. White holly and ebony work well enough together, but I do not consider ebony a hard wood. Of course there are many who will dispute this assertion, but it is easy enough to pick out specimens of any wood that are hard, but what I mean to say is, that, in general, it is not a truly hard wood, like rosewood or even cocoanut. White holly is almost as soft as pine, and contrasts finely with the only natural black wood that we have. There is one other black wood, of which I have seen specimens, that is perfection

itself, so far as color, grain, and strength are con-
cerned. Indeed, it can scarcely be said to have a
grain, so firm and solid is it in texture. It turns
like horn, or ivory, and is of the "darkest, deep-
est, deadliest," black. Unfortunately, I cannot
give the name of it, for the reason that the gentle-
man who gave it to me, did not know himself
what it was, and he obtained it from the captain
of a vessel trading to Africa.*

Mere white and black wood, side by side, do
not look well unless some kind of pattern or design is observed, and if the pattern is obtained
only at great expense of time and labor, it is also
unsatisfactory. I shall show, further along, how
different designs can be produced rapidly and accurately, with but comparatively little labor.

By inlaying, too, many most beautiful designs
can be produced, with but little labor compared
to that which is generally bestowed upon such
work. This kind of ornamentation is beautiful
upon work tables, work boxes, cigar stands, paper
knives, fan handles, fancy boxes, inkstands, card
cases, vases, picture frames, penholders, sleeve
buttons, ear-rings, chess and checker men, napkin
rings, fancy drawer knobs, jewel caskets, watch
holders, glove boxes, in fact, the whole array of

*I have since learned that it is called African "Black Thorn."

9

fine cabinet work, looks better when neatly and tastefully inlaid with woods that match and harmonize with the subject, and with each other. I think that some of the methods I practice are new to most persons, and I am sure they will be found accurate and expeditious; which last is a point of no small importance; for when a person works a long time over an elaborate thing, he gets terribly tired of it after while, if it is slow and plodding. In fact, where there is much that is uniform in character, as in making a check pattern, in black and white colors in squares, not over the tenth of one inch wide—it is impossible to make any thing like regularity, or fine fitting, and close joints, by handling each piece separately.

I therefore have a variety of what I call "stock" on hand, ready laid up, in all colors and dimensions, so that I can choose from it exactly as I would pick out a tool. This stock consists of wood laid up in the patterns shown in Figs. 59–67, and of sizes varying according to my designs, but generally very near the sizes here shown.

These are laid up in long strips, say twelve inches long, or as may be conveniently handled. They are all sawed out with a fine circular saw, by some one who understands cutting hard wood for this purpose. The stuff must be shoved

through the saw with a very regular, gradual
feed, so as to cut a smooth surface, and if the saw
is not right for cutting smooth on the side, it
must be made so; for it will not do to plane the
strips after they are sawed, as there never would
be any uniformity between them, and the joints

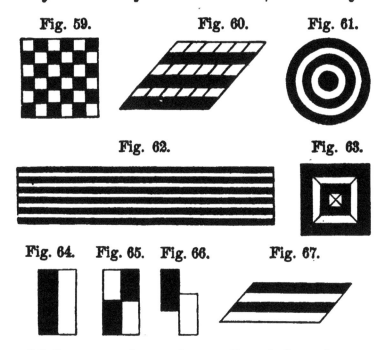

Fig. 59.   Fig. 60.   Fig. 61.

Fig. 62.   Fig. 63.

Fig. 64.   Fig. 65.   Fig. 66.   Fig. 67.

would be very imperfect. In gluing them up,
there is nothing particular to be observed, except
that the glue must be very hot, laid on well with
a stiff brush, and the stuff clamped between two
thick boards, which have been planed perfectly
true on the faces; so that the union will be perfect
between the strips. In this way the job will be

well done, and the sections will show uniformly. As it is the sections that are mainly used, this is a matter of great importance; for when it is necessary to have an ornamental border to a work-box, for example, it is only requisite to saw off as many sections, from the end of any of the blocks, as may be desired; as in Fig. 68. It is then a

Fig. 68.

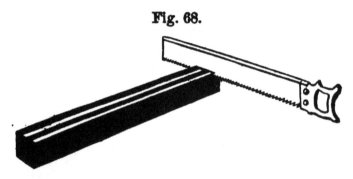

simple and easy thing to lay them in, one after another, in the place that has been left for them.

I do not saw off each square strip by itself before I glue the stock, but I lay up several flat pieces, as in Fig. 69, which represents one *end*

Fig. 69.

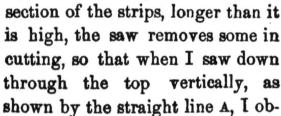

section of the strips, longer than it is high, the saw removes some in cutting, so that when I saw down through the top vertically, as shown by the straight line A, I obtain square strips in long pieces, but all glued together so they are easy to handle, these I afterward glue together again, so that white and black alternate, as in the checker-board, and I then have the pattern precisely uniform in all the length of the stock. I claim originality for this plan, and also expedition in execution; more than either I get entire uniformity. Of course it is easy to make any other pattern in the same way, and it is surprising to see how many rectangular and acute-angled patterns can be made with these sections. It is sometimes possible to get veneers of the right thickness, but any veneer cutter will saw the wood as desired.

ꞌ Since the paragraph above was written, I have seen some "Tunbridge Ware" work made in England, which is, I am sure, done in the same way. Therefore, I am not the originator of the idea, but I can certify that it is a good and a quick way of making very elaborate patterns.

9*

CHAPTER XV.

STAMP INLAYING.

OF course there are times and places where the sameness and rigidity of angular patterns are tedious, and the eye and hand, fatigued by it, desire a change into something more graceful and harmonious in effect. The smaller the pattern, the more tedious, irksome, and expensive the goods. To avoid delay is one object of the workman, but to obtain perfection is the chief. In order to do this, we must have some plan or some tool to multiply the same shape with great rapidity and regularity.

In fine workmanship, or rather in small pieces, it would be impossible to cut out any great number with the certainty of their being at all similar; some would be large, some small, and all different. Let us imagine that it is desired to inlay a laurel wreath, or a garland of stars in an elliptic pattern about the edge of a box cover, as in Fig. 70. It will be seen that to cut each one in with a chisel would be an endless task. I therefore propose to do it much quicker than it can be done by other plan, and that is by a stamp. I make a

Fig. 70.

steel stamp, or punch, of the exact size of the
pattern I wish to let in the box, and am careful to
have it bevel inwards, from the edges toward the
top, as in Fig. 71, not only to avoid breaking
down the edges, but to make a clean, sharp impression in the
wood. It is ne-
cessary to cut in
pretty deep, for,

Fig. 71.

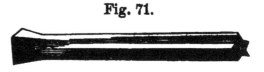

with all your care, you cannot avoid breaking the
edge to some extent, and it can only be practised on

any solid, sound wood, *not veneered.* Except for
large patterns, I do not put veneers in these incisions, or stamp markings, as I could not cut them
out so small, as the pattern shows in the engraving, but I either make a cement of white lead, and
push that into the holes, or, using the same
stamp I cut in the pattern in the wood with, I cut
pieces out of thin sheet German silver, and push
them in with great ease. If I use silver, I am
careful to cut in below the surface of the cover
on the box, so that I can put the cover in the
lathe again, and refinish the top so as to be flush
with the silver. In this way I get a true, uniform,
and even pattern, which looks as if it had grown
in its place; for grace and elegance of appearance,
it cannot be surpassed. Where it is absolutely
necessary to use a chisel and cutting tool to inlay
with, I still make stamps, even so large as half an
inch superficial area, for they are soon cut out,
and serve to mark the outlines for the chisel, so
that it is easier to cut the pattern by their aid.

In straight lines, or even in letting in circles,
parts of circles, ellipses, in fact, any curved or
angular work with veneers, I invariably cut the
pattern *out* before laying it on the box, and then
fit the other colored pieces in the spaces left.
Very many veneers cannot be handled at all when
dry, without breaking all to pieces and spoiling

the pattern. It will be necessary to soak ebony, for instance, for some time before you want to use it. With this precaution, you can cut it in any shape without danger. It is the same with maple veneer. When I have cut out an intricate pattern in ebony, and wish to inlay the same with holly, I obtain an exact duplicate of the shape the holly should have, by placing it, *wet*, over the ebony, holding it firmly, so that it cannot slip, and then rapping the holly with the end of a tool handle. In this way a fac simile of the pattern is transferred in wet lines to the holly, and you have only to follow them over with a lead pencil to get a perfect shape. Then take a sharp square-ended knife, and laying the veneer on a hard surface, cut slowly and carefully all round the marks, and after a few incisions, you will have the satisfaction of seeing it come out perfect.

CHAPTER XVI.

DESIGNS IN MOSAIC.

THESE methods greatly expedite the *labor* of inlaying, for mere labor much of it is; that is, when repetition of the pattern is frequent, as it is in small designs.

The great trouble and vice of amateur mechanics is *haste;* they are too anxious to see the result of a design to give it proper attention in detail, and, as a consequence, it lacks that nicety and uniform elegance that characterize the shop-made goods. For where men work by the day, they are not too energetic as a rule.

DESIGNS IN MOSAIC.

By this I mean the employment of small bits of different colored woods to produce a certain effect. I have seen many that were made to represent foliage of trees, the wood being stained green, of course, but these works of art seem to me labor thrown away, and, except as mere curiosities, are in no wise attractive; for no workman can do more than *imitate* nature in this line, and it is a poor imitation.

A legitimate branch of this line of work is that wherein small bits, say of the size of Fig. 72, can be conveniently used. When laid in nicely, and the colors arranged to harmonize, they certainly look well, resembling the straw flower work, or inlaid straw work of Japan. The wood may be dyed any color desired, but it is much nicer to use those colored by nature, which do not fade. I give here a list of naturally colored woods, useful for this kind of work.

Fig. 72.

Black—Ebony.
Red—Cam Wood, Tulip Wood.
Yellow—Boxwood.
White—Holly.
Brown—Walnut, Cocoa.
Red Brown—Spanish Cedar (cigar box).

These woods all inlay well except the Spanish Cedar and Walnut, which are apt to chip and sliver off on the edges, when cut thin. Cam wood is a pretty red wood, very close in grain, but not to be had in veneers, as it is used chiefly for making dyes. Most of this kind of work looks better when ranged in angles about a center, though I recently saw a work-box in Boston, which had an accurate representation of a worsted

pattern worked on a canvas, but as the workman
had unfortunately selected a very ugly pattern,
and the woods had faded, his labor was wholly
thrown away.

After having arranged or laid one course in
mosaic work, it is comparatively easy to follow
the whole around, but it is absolutely essential
that the pieces to be let in should be fac similes
of each other, for unless this is the case, the pattern
will come out wrong when the ends are joined, or
where it meets.   Great care must be observed in
this, and as it would be almost impossible to cut
slips of veneer so small, and be accurate, I prefer
to take a slip of wood, and saw off of the end,
having, of course, previously planed and calli-
pered the stick perfectly true.   Here let me say,
that the saw I use for this purpose, is the watchmakers' dividing saw, the same as jewellers use.
Some of the saws are scarcely larger than a horse
hair, while others are three-tenths of an inch deep
and very narrow.   With this instrument I can
work very delicately as regards thinness and
smoothness of surface.   It is also admirable for
scroll sawing, of which more hereafter.

Of course, all these are small jobs, and small,
fine work; when it comes to more elaborate patterns, such as a regenerally found on tables, work-
boxes, musical boxes, and similar things, it re-

quires more time, but as the pattern is large, it requires no particular patience beyond that which
a *very* fine piece of work does. But where the
pieces are small, as in mosaic, it takes a great deal
of patience to pick up one after another, and no
small degree of artistic talent to bring them all in
in the right place.

10

CHAPTER XVII.

FINISHING THE OUTSIDE.

WHEN the pattern has all been laid, the next thing that remains is to finish the exterior, and polish it or oil it as may be desired. To do this it is, of course, necessary to use great care. The veneers, if they have been used, are very thin, about the twenty-fifth part of an inch, and there is not much to come off. It must therefore be scraped very carefully with a sharp scraper, either in the lathe, or, if the work be a flat surface, by a scraper held in the hand, and made of sheet steel of the best quality. In using the scraper, care must be taken to humor the grain of the wood, so that it will not be roughened up by being rubbed the wrong way. When it has been scraped sufficiently smooth, it must be thoroughly rubbed with sand paper, until it has an even, uniform surface all over. If it is to be varnished and polished, French polish as it is termed, such as is seen on pianos, it will require a long time and much experience to make it a success. The reason is this: the polish is really given to the gum of which the varnish is composed, and not to the wood itself. The gum sinks into the pores of the wood and fills them up, and hardens as it is applied, but the fluids in which the gums are dissolved, either turpentine or oil, evaporate comparatively slowly, so that before each coat is applied, the previous one must be dry and hard, or else the next one will be streaky, and the surface will be ridgy.

The length of time depends greatly on the weather; from three to six months being required to properly dry and harden a piano-case so that it will wear—six months is, however, extreme, and is only the case in very warm weather. It will easily be seen why so many amateurs fail in producing that vitreous glaze, or polish, which is so universally admired. Not one in fifty has patience enough to wait until the first coat dries, before the second is applied, and they keep trying the varnish, to see if it won't work, in a day or two after it has been put on. It sometimes takes ten days before the third coat is ready to apply the next. It is a common fault to apply too much varnish on the first coat. It is necessary to rub it into the grain of the wood, so that it is thoroughly charged with it, and sinks into the pores. By rubbing it is merely meant to take a little on the brush and cover the surface gradually, without trying to make it look well or ill. The ground work has to be put on first, before any thing can be done toward ornamenting. After one coat has been put on, it must be rubbed down with sand paper to remove any varnish that may not have sunk into the work, and when all is fair and smooth and dry, a second coat may be applied and treated in the same way. The third coat may be applied rather more freely, and must be left to get thorougly hard before treating it. It must then be rubbed freely with pumice stone flour, and water. This will leave it bright and hard if the varnish has been skillfully put on, and a coat of flowing varnish may now be put on for the last. Flowing varnish is so-called because it is lighter in body than most varnishes, and is intended as the last of all, to produce that elegant glossy surface which characterizes all fine work.

Many persons use shellac varnish, which is simply gum lac (the proper name is " lac "), which is a gum found in the Indies; the trade give it the names of shell-lac and seed-lac, and one other which I have forgotten: shell-lac is the kind used for varnish. The gum is simply dissolved in alcohol of high proof; the solution being aided by exposure to a warm place and agitation from time to time. As this varnish dries immediately, or within an hour, owing to the rapid evaporation of the alcohol; it is very convenient for amateurs who are of an energetic turn of mind, and wish to see their productions turned and finished in a breath, as one may say. It takes a fair polish, but is by no means so durable or beautiful as copal or hard varnishes. On some woods, as, for instance, cherry, pine, or cedar, it is very appropriate, and looks well.

It is quite easy to write these instructions and observations down, but there is a dexterity, acquired only by practice, which cannot be told to any one, and the operator must, if possible, inform himself by visiting the nearest cabinet or piano factory, and see with his eyes for himself.

I should have said previously that ivory black introduced into shell-lac varnish, gives a very good black lacquer, closely imitating japan, while other colors, such as blue, carmine, green, or yellow, have the effect of enamel when handsomely rubbed down and polished with several coats. I have seen some most beautiful knobs for drawers, fancy handles, etc., made in this way, that looked like porcelain.

Oiled wood looks well in furniture, and there may be some who desire to use it on fancy work. It is simply linseed oil applied in successive coats; but it requires time to dry, and always has a disagreeable odor about it.

10*

CHAPTER XVIII.

INLAYING CONTINUED.

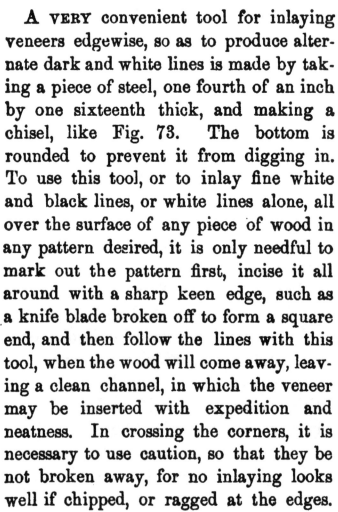

Fig. 73. A VERY convenient tool for inlaying veneers edgewise, so as to produce alternate dark and white lines is made by taking a piece of steel, one fourth of an inch by one sixteenth thick, and making a chisel, like Fig. 73. The bottom is rounded to prevent it from digging in. To use this tool, or to inlay fine white and black lines, or white lines alone, all over the surface of any piece of wood in any pattern desired, it is only needful to mark out the pattern first, incise it all around with a sharp keen edge, such as a knife blade broken off to form a square end, and then follow the lines with this tool, when the wood will come away, leaving a clean channel, in which the veneer may be inserted with expedition and neatness. In crossing the corners, it is necessary to use caution, so that they be not broken away, for no inlaying looks well if chipped, or ragged at the edges.

This is especially convenient for drawing lines across mahogany boxes that have been put together before inlaying was thought of for them. The veneers should all be glued together, side and side first, that is, if two colors are used, then they will fit on the ends properly, and may be handled with more expedition.

GLUING IN VENEERS.

In a previous part of this little work I have advised the use of waterproof cements for fine inlaying, so that dampness will not affect them, but as this is not always convenient, it is well to make the glue so that it can be used and the work finished off in a short time. This is easily done by making the glue as thick as it will run, or so that it is like a jelly. If applied in this condition, it will set hard in thirty minutes, and the work may be cut down without fear or danger of its moving. I have done this frequently, in order to see what kind of work I was making. Always put a clamp on your work wherever you can, for although the glue will adhere of itself to the wood, it adheres much more strongly if pressed down by a clamp. Also, never put a veneer on a piece of work that is uneven, for although it may set square under the pressure of the clamp, when you come to scrape it, it will give way and yield to the inequalities, and when varnished and polished, will be full of depressions.

Don't be afraid to rub down with sand paper, under the impression that you are spoiling the work, but let the varnish get thoroughly dried, and be hard before you attempt it. Be sure, also, to remove every particle of varnish if you touch it at all, otherwise that which remains will take a coat while the bare wood will not take so much, and you will have a surface full of scars and ridges. It is not necessary to touch the wood in rubbing down, but go down *to* the wood, so that a waxy appearance is presented, and you will have a handsome finish that will add greatly to the beauty of the work. White holly is easily soiled when used in connection with ebony, by the dust from it, and it will be necessary to rub it, or scrape it delicately, before varnishing, without touching the ebony.

IVORY.

This substance is certainly a most attractive one to the turner. Pure in color, hard, solid and strong beyond belief in texture or grain, it has the fewest disadvantages of any substance we use. It is easily dyed to any shade, and will hold it a long while. Either for jewelry, or rather for personal adornment, or articles of utility, it is well adapted, and but for the cost of it would be in general use. It is getting dearer and scarcer each year. The best comes from Ceylon, and that in least repute from African elephants; the former is said to be much stronger and more solid.

Of its general manipulation there is not much to be said, except that the workman will find it trying to the edge of his tools. In all respects it can be cut and turned like hard woods.

Fig. 74.

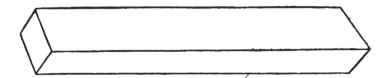

It is easily softened by immersion for a time in weak acid, so that its friability, toughness, or tendency to resist the carving tool, is destroyed, and this without injuring the goods, unless the acid is too strong.

As it is so expensive in general, it is well for the amateur to know that he can purchase it in all shapes, either in squares like Fig. 74, or in flat, cord-like slips, from dealers in it. I will mention one person, F. Grote, 78 Fulton street, New York, who generally has a good assortment of this kind.

It is extremely convenient to find pieces of the exact size and shape one needs, and it is also economical, both in time and material, for all ivory must be sawed, and that is slow work where there are no facilities. After the article, whatever it may be, is turned, it may be either dyed, or polished in its natural color.

POLISHING.

This is performed in the easiest way. A wet rag will polish ivory, but in order to put on a brilliant gloss, take starch, or Spanish white, saturate a wet rag with it, and hold it on the work; when dried off and rubbed with a woolen cloth or a piece of chamois leather, it will have a brilliant and durable gloss.

DYEING IVORY.

I tried a great many plans and recipes for dyeing ivory before I hit upon any that were in all respects satisfactory. Most of them were nasty, involved the purchase of drugs and dyes that were sure to be adulterated, and the results were vexatious, but one day, in dyeing some silk with family dye color, prepared by Howe and Stevens, of Boston, Massachusetts, the idea occurred to me to try it on ivory. It succeeded to admiration, and I had found what I had so long sought, namely, a clean, cheap, simple and *sure* method of coloring ivory to any shade needed, in a short time. The color can always be had, ready for use, in any town, as much so as a bottle of ink, while the various shades and gradations of tint are ready made to hand; there is no need of stale urine, or any other mess,—simple immersion in the hot liquid from ten to twenty-four hours will give a permanent and brilliant hue to any article. I have never seen such brilliant colors as these dyes give. The solferino and the black are particularly handsome, and are insoluble in water; that is, the goods may be washed without injury. The solferino will not bear *hard* rubbing in water, but the black and other colors will, without injury. The depth to which the color penetrates depends upon the length of time the goods are immersed, but twenty-four hours, and even six hours in some cases, will answer all purposes. For chessmen, the solferino is a splendid color, while all the other tints can be had for other kinds of fancy work.

Ivory is particularly suitable for mosaic inlaying, as it never chips, and can be cut into the smallest and thinnest pieces without danger of fracture. It will hold on wood with glue, though there are other cements, stronger, for the purpose.

It can also be dyed before inlaying, and afterwards rubbed down to a uniform surface, but the work must be done well, as the dyes do not always penetrate equally, and if the work is delicate and the design small, it is apt to change the colors to rub them down.   Napkin rings, breast pins, masonic mallets and emblems generally, miniature gothic chairs with carved backs for ornamental purposes, chess and checker men, small boxes for lip and eye salves, needle cases, thimble cases, ring and jewel boxes, penholders, silk-winders card cases, all afford a fine opportunity for the skill and taste of the amateur.

CHAPTER XIX.

ORNAMENTAL DESIGNS FOR INLAYING.

ALTHOUGH a handsomely veined piece of wood is as beautiful a thing as any one would wish to see, there are occasionally pieces of work that look well inlaid, and for this it is desirable that we should have as pretty patterns and judiciously chosen woods and contrasts as we can get.

I give here what I think is a pretty design for the cover of a round box. It is easily made, and I venture to suggest that the following colors will will be found agreeable; No. 1, tulip with out-side edge of white holly, tulip to be cut across the grain. No. 2, ebony cut out of a solid veneer, that is not pieced. It will save a great deal of time and labor to glue this veneer on to mahogany a quarter of an inch thick, and then saw the pattern out with a fine turn-saw. To get the veneer off whole, soak it in warm water for a few minutes. No. 3, boxwood. No. 4, ebony. No. 5, tulip, or, if you can get it, turtle wood. It is sometimes to be had of Henry A. Kerr, Center street, New York, dealer in woods. The

11

central flower can be omitted or executed. It is a good deal of work, but will make a beautiful piece when well done. Turtle wood is very remarkable, being yellow inclining to salmon, mottled with brownish black streaks, sometimes black with superb crimson markings, like a summer sunset after a thunder storm.

Fig. 76 is another similar pattern. Of course the workman will make such disposition of the colors as he pleases. When these are varnished and French polished, they certainly look splendidly, and are specimens of work that any one may be proud of; of course supposing them to be well fitted as to joints, and without the glairy, sticky appearance that characterizes varnish half rubbed down, and that worked before it has hardened. Hardening and drying are two different things. Varnish dries before it hardens, and requires time, the more the better, to season, so it can be polished. This is a very easy pattern to fit, and any one of experience can make it complete in four or six hours.

Fig. 77 is still another pattern, but what is shown dark, as at A, in the outer circles should be light to represent tulip wood. Tulip contrasts splendidly with ebony. The center or body of the cover should be rosewood. This must be put on first, all over the whole surface, and a white holly ring put on the outside edge. The exterior and interior circles, which form the pattern, are then cut out by a tool like a carpenter's bit used in the lathe, as in this diagram. The letter *a* is round, and will, of course, make a slight center hole in the box cover, but as it is covered up that is a matter of no moment. The inner circles B should also be tulip, or some wood that contrasts with ebony; mahogany is very handsome. This pattern is not pretty, but it is striking and unique, which is sometimes the same thing. Of course, the distances of the circles must be determined beforehand with a pair of compasses.

In scroll sawing much can be done that is pleasing to the eye in small works, but for large designs and intricate ones, the amateur will find an upright or jig saw necessary, unless he be more than usually patient.

For the joints of boxes before veneering I always prefer screws rather than dovetailing, which takes a long time, and is no better when done; screws are sure, never start, and save time, which is a great consideration with amateurs, whose tasks are often, indeed, in nearly all cases, carried on after some other labor is over, in the interim between arduous toil.

White woods, such as holly, need white glue, else the joints will show. Beware of dust in your varnish brush, and take care that you soak it for half a day before using it, else the hairs will come out on your work and ruin it. Flat, camel's hair brushes are to be used, and can be had in every paint store. Use only the whitest copal varnish for your white holly, else you will find it yellow holly after the varnish has been put on. Most varnishes need thinning slightly with turpentine before use, especially if they have been kept some time.

Keep your lathe centers so that they run true on the points at all times, and have a mark on them so that they always enter from the same side of the lathe mandrel.

When you put clamps on to hold your veneers, as you always should, be careful, if your wood is soft, that you do not set the clamps so tight as to sink the veneer into the lower wood, for the result will be an uneven surface, that nothing can remedy.

Be careful to have clean glue and clean surfaces if you wish to make sound work. Dust or grit ruins glue so that it will not hold.

CHAPTER XX.

GENERAL SUMMARY.

IN polishing metals, whether brass, iron, steel, or of whatever nature, it is essential that the tool marks and scratches of files, or other agents, should be entirely removed before the final gloss is given, otherwise the work will have a cheap look that detracts very much from its appearance.

If emery of the finest character (flour) is used, with oil, the result will be very beautiful, but this makes a mess about the lathe it is desirable to avoid. Polish with oil is softer in appearance than dry polishing, and is much more durable, being not so liable to rust and tarnish. Dry polishing is performed with sand paper of various grades, running from $\frac{1}{2}$ to 0. This gives a very bright, dazzling finish, that is easily rusted. Brass must be treated with rotten stone and oil to be nicely polished, and after this the burnisher should be used. Lacquers are employed for the purpose of preserving the polish unimpaired, and are made as follows:

11*

LACQUERS.

2 gals. Alcohol, proof, specific gravity not less than 95 per. cent.

1 lb. Seed-lac.

1 oz. Gum Copal.

1 oz. English Saffron.

1 oz. Annotto.

Another.

40 ozs. Proof Alcohol.

8 grs. Spanish Annotto.

2 drs. Turmeric.

½ oz. Shellac.

12 grs. Red Sanders.

When dissolved add 30 drops Spirit of Turpentine.

Directions for Making.—Mix the ingredients, and let the vessel containing them stand in the sun, or in a place slightly warmed, for three or four days, shaking it frequently till the gum is dissolved, after which let it settle from 24 to 48 hours, when the clear liquor may be poured off for use. Pulverized glass is sometimes used in making lacquers, to carry down the impurities.

The best burnisher is a piece of bloodstone ground to shape and set in a handle ; they can be bought for about a dollar and a half at any watchmakers' tool store. Rouge powder is also an excellent thing for polishing brass and German silver. German silver, in wire, also in sheet, can be had at the same place.

For silver plating fluid the workman will find that manufactured by Howe & Stevens, Boston, Massachusetts, to be the best of its class, as it leaves a thin coating of pure silver on the metal, which can be renewed from time to time, as it wears, by a fresh application.

Any articles that require to be gilt can be best done by electro platers, who will deposit as much gold on the surface as one desires, even to the thirty-second part of an inch. It is better, however, to buy a small battery, which can be had for four or five dollars, and do this for yourself. Very many other things can be electro-plated, and fac-similes of medals produced at a small cost, which will be both instructive and ornamental.

SOLDERING.

There are many ways of soldering, but the amateur will find the spirit lamp and the soldering iron the most convenient and expeditious.

In soldering tinned surfaces, no particular care is needed, as the solder will adhere easily, but in brass, or other metals, it does not do so without the aid of a rosin flux or acid solution. These simply act to make the surfaces chemically clean, so that the solder will hold. In fact, cleanliness is absolutely indispensable to success, for the solder will crawl off of any thing that is dirty or greasy, even though it may not appear to be so. Lead and tin are used for solder, and can be bought of any tinner very cheaply. The end of the soldering iron (which is not iron, but copper, by the way) should be tinned, otherwise the solder will not hold on it, neither will it follow when the iron is drawn along a seam.

The iron is readily tinned in this way. File it to the shape you want it, and put it in the fire, heating it pretty hot, but nothing like redness. You are then to wipe it clean quickly on a rag wet with soldering fluid, which can be had in drug stores, and is made of muriatic acid and sheet zinc dissolved in the same; the zinc must be clean, and in small strips, and shaken gradually until dissolved. The solution must then be well diluted with water. It is used by wetting the rag aforesaid with it and rubbing the iron in it; if block tin in strips be now rubbed on the end of the iron, it will adhere, and the iron will be ready for use. The iron must not be heated so as to melt off the tin and expose the copper underneath; for the iron is then useless until tinned again.

The soldering fluid is always to be used when brass, or any surfaces not coated with tin, are to be united,

By the spirit lamp you can join metallic surfaces very easily and quickly as follows: take your plate, or whatever it is you wish to join together, and scour it bright with fine sand-paper or pumice stone and water, on the faces to be united. Apply the soldering fluid, hold it over the spirit lamp blaze, and as soon as it is well heated, rub it over with a stick of tin; when it is well tinned, lay it on a hot flat iron or the stove for a minute, until you have tinned the other piece, then clap both together, and they will set instantly.

The blowpipe is very convenient for soldering small pieces together that cannot be touched with the iron, but as it requires some skill to use it, the amateur is not likely to be very successful with it. The articles to be soldered in this way, should be placed on a piece of charcoal, so that the heat will be equally distributed and kept up during the process.

VARNISHING AND POLISHING.

On no account is a second coat of varnish to be applied before the first one is dry. If this *is* done the result will be a sticky, ridgy, dirty looking job. Before the work is varnished even, it must be thoroughly sandpapered to remove inequalities, and the last sandpapering should be with the finest grade. Then apply the varnish, taking care not to put too much on for the first coat. When that is dry and *hard*, sandpaper with fine paper again and varnish again. Three to four coats are enough for ordinary work. When the last coat is dry and hard, get some floated pumice stone flour, that is, pumice stone flour that has been washed, mix it with water to about the thickness of cream; apply it to a woolen rag, and rub it gently over the work; not too hard, for that would cut the varnish off down to the wood. After a while you will see that the surface of the varnish begins to have a hard, smooth body, like carriage work. When this occurs, you can wash the pumice stone all off, and take a little Tripoli or rotten stone and oil, and rub gently all over the job; you will then have a surpassingly beautiful and brilliant surface, that will show the grain and vein of the wood to perfection. If you desire the gloss that varnish gives, you must apply a thin coat of wearing varnish after this, In varnishing, you must buy " rubbing varnish " if you intend to polish and oil varnish, not spirit, which is apt to crack and rub up under the treatment.

BRUSHES.

In varnishing, you, of course, desire to have a true and even surface, without a ridge to show where the brush left it. Camel's hair flat brushes are used for this purpose, but they will not answer in spirit varnishes, as the hairs drop out or are loosened from the action of the spirit on the shellac or glue, which holds them in. Bristle brushes are the best for general use. They must be soaked for an hour or more in cold water, to fasten the bristles before using.

PEARL.

This substance is easily sawed into shape, and is easily turned with a common steel tool. It is polished readily with pumice stone and water and "putty powder," this last to be had of chemists or lapidaries. It is better to preserve the colored surface as nature left it, for the beautiful rays and tints presented by it are owing to a peculiar disposition of thin scales on the surface, which retain the light; if these be destroyed, the beauty of the material is lost. It is to be had of marine store keepers generally, or the amateur can get it more readily of the nearest button manufacturer.

MISCELLANEOUS TOOLS.

If you buy any tools, always buy the best that money can get. P. S. Stubs' files, wire, rimmers, and screw plates, are standard tools, and the amateur cannot go astray in choosing them. A vise is indispensable, and it should be large enough to hold the work without springing.

CURVING MAPLE VENEERS.

If you wish to curve a veneer so that it will fit a half or a whole circle, it is easily done by dipping it iu hot water, when it will instantly curl up into any shape you want. I do this with bird's eye maple. This wood is easily stained any hue, and is rather handsomer in chocolate brown than in its natural color. It is then the nearest to French oak of any wood that we have, and that is unquestionably superb. Such markings and mottlings as it has, surpass anything ever seen; it is a deep, rich, chocolate brown color, full of snarls, curves, and knots, not over five eights of an inch in their largest diameters, and so beautiful that it seems as if some hand must have arranged them.

The French oak is susceptible of a splendid polish, but I am unable to say how it works, for I never worked any, nor do I know where to get it. Curled maple will also take a handsome dye. Get Howe & Stevens's Dye Colors in powder—they can be had in any apothecary's store, of any shade—put it in an earthen dish and boil it, then dip or sponge the veneer with it. The color will strike through and through, and you may sand-paper it as much as you please without removing it. It is a very beautiful job to take a plain ogee moulding and curl a bird's eye maple veneer on the round part, and an ebony veneer on the fillet or hollow, and then varnish and polish it. It makes one of the most beautiful picture frames that ever was seen; having all the effect of mouldings made from the solid wood.

CUTTING MISCELLANEOUS MATERIALS.

By these I mean horn jet, malachite, alabaster, cannel coal, glass, and similar substances. For all of these, except malachite, steel will answer, but that steel will not touch. It is not a nice material to work, being apt to check and crack in the most unlooked-for manner. To those who have never seen it, I will say that it is a stone, or species of marble, obtained in Russia, and is green in color, marked with white and greenish gray stripes. The green is specially brilliant, and the effect is very fine. Although it is so hard that steel will not cut it, it is easily scratched in use, and is a soft stone, and can be readily cut on a common vulcanite emery wheel, and polished on a razor strop covered with rouge powder. It is frequently used for jewelry. Glass is easily filed in a lathe with a common file, but I do not know what any one should wish to work glass for, as it is exceedingly dangerous from the splinters which fly from it, is quite friable and easily broken, and is, moreover, so common that no value attaches to it. Very pretty vases can be made out of alabaster by turning them in the lathe.

INDEX.

Lightning Source UK Ltd.
Milton Keynes UK
UKHW012028130722
405825UK00002B/27